"I'm sorry this happened to you."

His voice was gentle. Almost a whisper. And even though Rosalie figured that being in his arms was a very bad idea, she just didn't have the strength to push him away.

Austin made a soft shushing sound and eased her deeper into his arms. Until she was pressed against him. Even with the tears and her heart shattering, she felt his body. Heard the quick rhythm of his breath.

Just as when she had spotted him at the table with his bedroom hair and eye-catching jeans, the trickle of heat went through her. A bad kind of heat that she didn't want to feel for him. But felt, anyway.

Rosalie pulled in her breath, taking in his scent with it, and suddenly everything that happened couldn't compete with what she knew they were both feeling right at this moment.

KIDNAPPING IN KENDALL COUNTY

USA TODAY *Bestselling Author*

DELORES FOSSEN

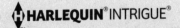

Recycling programs
for this product may
not exist in your area.

ISBN-13: 978-0-373-74855-6

Kidnapping in Kendall County

Copyright © 2014 by Delores Fossen

Printed in U.S.A.

www.Harlequin.com

ABOUT THE AUTHOR

USA TODAY bestselling author Delores Fossen has sold over fifty novels with millions of copies of her books in print worldwide. She's received the Booksellers' Best Award and the RT Reviewers' Choice Award, and was a finalist for a prestigious RITA® Award. In addition, she's had nearly a hundred short stories and articles published in national magazines. You can contact the author through her web-page at www.dfossen.net.

Books by Delores Fossen

CAST OF CHARACTERS

Rosalie McKinnon—A rancher's daughter who'll do anything to find her kidnapped baby, and that includes teaming up with a man who could cost her everything. Again.

Austin Duran—An FBI agent who's gone rogue to find his own missing nephew, but his search for the baby puts him on a collision course with Rosalie.

Sadie McKinnon—Rosalie's missing eleven-month-old daughter.

Sonny Buckland—A PI who might know a lot more about the kidnappings than he's admitting.

Trevor Yancy—A shady businessman who's already had a tragic run-in with Rosalie and Austin.

Vickie Cravens—A nanny who might have been duped by the kidnappers.

Seth Calder—Rosalie's stepbrother. To protect Rosalie, he's helping with the investigation.

Chapter One

Rosalie McKinnon tightened her grip on the Beretta that she'd stolen and stepped out of the house and onto the narrow back porch. She stayed in the shadows, away from the milky kitchen light that was stabbing through the darkness.

There was only a thin lip of an overhang on the roof, so after just a few steps, the December rain spat at her. Not sleet exactly, but close enough. Rosalie didn't know if she was shivering from the fear or the cold. It didn't matter. Shivering wasn't going to stop her.

Nothing would.

Tonight, she would get answers. Even if she had to shoot *him*.

She made it down the slick, uneven limestone steps and into the sprawling backyard. She paused just a couple of seconds to make sure no one in the house had noticed that she'd left. With all the decongestants and antihistamines she had managed to slip into the guard's coffee, maybe he'd be out long enough so he wouldn't realize that she was missing.

If not...

Well, best not to go there.

Even though she had stolen the guard's gun after he'd passed out, there were other armed guards on the grounds. If they discovered her, she'd be dead within seconds. Especially if they figured out what she was doing. They were no doubt capable of killing.

That also applied to the man she had to see.

Maybe, just maybe, he'd be sleeping, too, so she could get the jump on him. It was the only chance she had of making this plan work.

Hurrying now, Rosalie crossed the bare winter grass to a much smaller house at the back of the barn. Once, it'd probably been a guest cottage when the ranch was a real working operation. Now there was no livestock around, no hint of the life that'd once gone on here other than a tractor and hay baler that had been left to rust away. These days, the place was a glorified prison for the babies being processed for black market adoptions.

Since it made her sick to her stomach to think of that, Rosalie pushed the thought aside and tested the doorknob on the cottage.

Unlocked.

A big mistake on his part.

Rosalie opened the door and stepped inside. All dark and toasty warm. It smelled of too-strong coffee and the fast-food burgers that'd been brought in for their dinner.

The only light in the room of the cottage came from the kitchen in the main house, where she'd just been. It cut like slivers down the tiny front windows that were streaked with rain.

It took a couple of moments for Rosalie's eyes to adjust, and in the shadowy silhouettes, she saw a desk, a sofa and the small bed against the wall. There were two interior doors, both closed, and from what she'd learned from the guard's idle chatter, one was a bathroom. The other, a bedroom that was being used as a storage closet.

But it was the man on the bed who grabbed her full attention.

He was on his side, facing away from her. No cover on him, and he appeared to be wearing the same jeans and shirt he'd had on when she had spotted him earlier in the yard.

The guard had called him *boss.*

She'd yet to see him up close, but Rosalie had gotten another glimpse of him from the upstairs window of the main house. His dark brown Stetson had covered most of his face, but she'd watched to see where he would go. And he hadn't gone far—just to the cottage. All in all, it wasn't the worst place to confront a monster because he was alone here, away from the guards who would protect him.

Keeping the Beretta by her side, she walked closer, her heart thudding with each soft step. She had to remind herself to breathe. And to keep a clear head. Her instincts were to shoot, or run, but neither of those things would get her what she needed.

Too bad she wasn't a cop like her siblings. They would have no doubt handled this much better.

But then they would have never gotten into this place.

Not with their cops' eyes and attitudes. Plus, they'd all been tied up with other leads and other investigations. Important ones. Her mother was about to stand trial for first-degree murder, and while finding the baby was critical, so was the trial since her mother was facing the death penalty.

That's why she'd come up with her own plan several months ago while she was staying at her family's ranch. A plan that'd started with finding any info to get her inside this place or any other place that would possibly lead her to her daughter.

Rosalie leaned over and jammed the gun to the back of the man's head. "I want answers," she managed to say even though her throat clamped shut. Her voice had hardly any sound.

He moved, just a fraction. "Darlin'," he drawled.

Her shoulders snapped back, and it was that split second of shock that caused her breath and body to freeze.

The man reached out, lightning-fast, snagged her by the right hand and stripped her of the Beretta. In the same motion, he pulled her down onto the bed with him and rolled on top of her, pinning her beneath him.

That unfroze her.

Her heart jolted, throbbing in her ears, and Rosalie started to fight back. She couldn't just let this man kill her.

"Play along," he growled, his voice no longer a drawl but rather a whisper. "There's a camera."

She'd already brought up her knee to ram any part of him that she could reach, but she stopped. Stared at him. Well, she stared at what she could see of him, anyway.

"Rosalie," he muttered.

Mercy. How did he know her real name? She was using a fake ID with the name Mary Williams. If he was onto her, why hadn't he already told the guards?

"Who are you?" she tried to ask, but he put his hand over her mouth.

"I figured you'd drop by," he said. No longer a whisper, and the cocky drawl had returned. "I saw you eyeing me earlier from the window."

She had. She'd *eyed* him and committed everything she could see about him to memory from his sandy-brown hair to lanky build. He normally wore a shoulder holster, and judging from the bulge in the back of his coat, he had another gun tucked in the back waistband of his jeans.

And the keys.

Three of them.

They jangled from a metal ring hooked to his belt loop.

Rosalie believed one was for the truck she'd seen him driving, but one of the others was for the room inside the main house where she'd gotten a glimpse of computers and files. The room was always locked, and there was a camera mounted on the doorjamb, but she needed his keys to get a look at those files.

She glanced around, to try to see if there was indeed a camera here, but the room was too dark.

"Who are you?" she asked, shoving his hand from her mouth.

He pulled back, stared down at her, though she still couldn't clearly see his face. "You don't know?" But he didn't wait for an answer. He mumbled some really bad profanity, and his grip tightened on her wrists. "Why the hell are you here, anyway?"

He didn't shout it, but she had no trouble hearing the anger in his voice. Or maybe not anger, but something.

What was going on? She couldn't see enough of his face to recognize him, and that raspy whispered voice wasn't enough of a clue. He could be friend or foe, but clearly he fell into the latter category since he was the boss here.

So, what was her next move?

She hadn't thought beyond getting answers and then trying to escape, but clearly she hadn't expected this. Whatever *this* was.

"Did you come here to kill me?" he demanded, still whispering.

"If necessary."

Except a dead man couldn't tell her what she needed to know. But she would have pulled the trigger if it'd come down to it. Unfortunately, she no longer had a gun as a bargaining tool. She had only shaky hands. Shaky body, too, and her heart just kept pounding.

The moments crawled by. Him, still staring at her and obviously waiting for an explanation. The only sounds were the rain pinging against the window and their rough breaths.

"Pretend," he finally snapped.

Rosalie didn't get a chance to ask what the heck that meant before his mouth went to her neck. He nuzzled it, as if kissing her, but he was still mumbling profanity, and his jaw muscles were way too tight for this to be a real kissing session.

So, what was this? Some kind of act for the person on the other end of the camera? If so, why was he trying to cover for her?

"I'm not leaving without answers," Rosalie whispered. "And I want these babies safely out of here and back where they belong."

"Pretend we're having sex or you might not be leaving at all. You'll be dead. And so will I."

That was the only warning she got before the pretense went into full swing. He kneed her legs apart, yanking off her green scrub pants. He didn't touch her panties, thank goodness, and he threw the covers over them.

He fumbled between them, pretending to unzip his jeans before the fake thrusting started.

"If necessary?" he said, repeating her response to his question of *Did you come here to kill me?* "If you're not here for revenge, then why did you come?"

Revenge, yes, she wanted that. And justice. But more than those things, she just wanted answers.

It was impossible to think with everything

going on. The sex was fake, but it was still a man's body shoving against her. And then there was the fear. Obviously, this man knew her. Knew she was as phony as the sex they were having. So, why hadn't he shouted out for the guard?

Why hadn't he killed her?

After all, he had her gun and his.

"I'm looking for my baby," she said. Her mouth trembled. And she felt her heart breaking all over again.

He stopped moving, met her gaze. For a few seconds, anyway. Then, he let out a loud groan, the sound of a man who'd just reached a climax, and he collapsed against her.

"You had a child," he said. Not a question exactly but more like something a person would say when trying to piece things together.

She nodded. Bad idea. It caused her mouth to brush against his neck, and because his sex was still aligned with hers, she felt a stirring.

Yes, this was pretend, but his body was obviously having a hard time remembering that.

"I gave birth to a baby girl nearly a year ago." Eleven months. Six days. Heck, she knew the hours and minutes.

"Nearly a year ago," he repeated. "She was your fiancé's baby?"

Again, not a question that she'd expected.

Rosalie nodded and tried to tamp down the massive lump in her throat. Her eyes burned with tears that she couldn't cry. Tears wouldn't help her baby now.

"Sadie…that's what I named my daughter. She was born eight and a half months after my fiancé was murdered."

The memories of that day came. Of his shooting. That horrible flood of images that just didn't stop. So senseless. Her fiancé, Special Agent Eli Wells, had died because of a botched investigation, and Rosalie had wanted to die right along with him.

And then she'd learned she was pregnant.

The baby had saved her. Because she'd put all her love and emotions into surviving, into the pregnancy, so she could have the child of the man she'd loved.

"Someone stole Sadie from the hospital just a few hours after she was born," Rosalie added, "and I've been looking for her ever since."

His breath was thicker now, practically gusting. "She wouldn't be here. They only bring newborns here, and they've only used this place for a couple of months."

Yes, she knew that from the guard's ramblings before he'd actually dozed off from the meds that she had slipped him. "I thought there would be records on the computer in a locked room of the house."

"There are. But only for the babies being held at this location. You're sure the black market ring took your daughter?"

"No." And it hurt to admit that. She wasn't sure of anything, but she'd exhausted her leads and had gone with this different angle. "A criminal informant said there might be information here."

There was a lot more to it than that, but Rosalie didn't want to rehash everything it'd taken to bring her to this point. All the lies, the payoffs and the bogus identity she'd had to create.

"Why haven't you killed me?" she came out and asked. "And how do you know who I am?"

Again, he took his time, looking down at her as if trying to figure out what was going on. Rosalie was doing the same thing to him.

"What criminal informant did you use?" he asked, obviously dodging the questions.

Of all the things that were up in the air here, that didn't seem very important. "A guy from San Antonio. Lefty Markham."

He groaned, cursed and rolled off her and to his side. But he immediately pulled her against him. Face-to-face. Like a couple having some pillow talk after a round of sex.

"He's your stepbrother's CI," he whispered. "Why the hell didn't you bring Seth in on this?"

Seth Calder, not just her stepbrother but also an FBI agent. So, not only did this man know who she was, but he also knew details about her life that he shouldn't know.

"Because Seth's checking out another lead over in El Paso. The CI said the baby-holding area here at the ranch wouldn't be here much longer."

"It won't be. The plan is to move tomorrow."

Oh, mercy. So soon. "I need to see those records. Please help me. *Please.*"

Yes, she was begging but she would resort to a lot more than that to learn where her baby had been taken.

"I'm Austin Duran," he said.

His voice was so soft, barely audible, but it slammed through her as if he'd yelled it.

"Oh, God," she said a lot louder than a whisper.

"Yeah." He moved away from her so they were no longer touching.

The name was as familiar to her as her own. But not in a good way. It was a name she'd cursed. A bogeyman who'd robbed her of her hopes and dreams.

The man who'd killed Eli.

Not in the eyes of the law, though, and it certainly hadn't been labeled murder. But Rosalie knew that Austin Duran was the FBI agent who had botched the investigation that'd led to Eli's murder.

"Yeah," he repeated. There was a lot of emotion hanging on that one word. The pain. The memories.

Everything Rosalie was feeling.

"You thought I'd come here to kill you," she mumbled. "You thought I was avenging Eli's death."

He didn't confirm that. Didn't need to.

"I didn't get a good look at your face." And that's why she hadn't instantly recognized him. Strange that she hadn't sensed that he had been so close, because she'd spent all these months hating him.

And Rosalie would use that hate.

In fact, it could be better than a gun.

"You're here undercover?" she asked.

He nodded. "I'm looking for…someone."

She didn't care about that. Didn't care about anything right now but her daughter. That included choking back her hatred for this man and making this work for Sadie and the other babies who were being held inside so they could be sold like cattle.

"You owe me," she insisted. "For Eli's death. And you're going to help me find his missing baby."

Austin didn't jump to do just that. He lay there, silent as death, and Rosalie was about to repeat her demand when she heard the sound.

Something she definitely didn't want to hear.

Footsteps.

Those steps were the only warning they got before there was another sound. The door flew open, and Austin scrambled in front of her.

But it was too late.

Two armed guards hurried into the cottage, and both pointed assault rifles at them.

Chapter Two

Austin had already spent the past twenty minutes or so cursing fate. And cursing Rosalie's untimely arrival in the cottage. It wouldn't do any good, but now he cursed the guards and those rifles trained on him.

"What the hell do you two want?" Austin growled, and he made a show of zipping up his jeans.

Austin didn't know the guys' names. Over the past week since he'd been undercover at the ranch, the flow of guards had stayed steady, none of them remaining in place for more than forty-eight hours. But it didn't matter what they called themselves. Austin just needed to get them out of there.

"Well?" Austin added in his worst snarl. He made sure he sounded like the person in charge.

He wasn't.

Heck, he didn't even know who had that particular title of being in charge or who exactly was watching him on the camera. However, it was pretty clear that someone had gotten suspicious of Rosalie's visit. The mock sex hadn't fooled them, and if Austin didn't do something fast to diffuse the situation, it could go from bad to worse.

The pair of guards exchanged glances as if trying to figure out what to do, but the guy on the right had a communicator in his ear, so he was no doubt receiving instructions.

"Why is she here?" The goon on the right tipped his head to Rosalie.

Austin gave him as cocky and flat of a look as he could manage. "Why do you think?"

"She's supposed to be inside," he snapped.

"The babies are asleep," Rosalie volunteered as if that explained everything.

It didn't, of course.

There were two newborns inside, along with a nanny and the guard. Since Rosalie had no doubt been hired as a nurse, she should have been inside and nowhere near Austin's quarters.

"I'll be going," Rosalie mumbled. She fished around on the floor for her scrub pants and pulled them on. She also pushed her long blond hair from her face.

Austin noticed that both her voice and hands were shaking, but hopefully the guards would think that was a reaction from being caught in the act of a lover's tryst. And nothing else.

Soon, if they got out of this, he'd need to convince Rosalie to leave so he could get on with his investigation.

This was a *bad* place for her to be.

She started for the door, but the men blocked her path. And they didn't lower those rifles. "You two know each other?" one of them asked.

"We do now." Austin shot her a sly smile. "But I'm ready for her to leave. Gotta get some sleep."

And he waited.

The guards still didn't move, though he could hear some chatter on the one guard's earpiece. Austin wished he could snap his fingers and make the real boss appear so they could settle this man-to-man, but so far he didn't have even a description of the person responsible for so much pain.

"Walk her back to the house," one of the guards finally said to Austin. "Make sure she stays put."

Austin tried not to look or sound too relieved, but he was. Rosalie and he had just dodged a bullet or two.

For now, anyway.

The real boss obviously didn't trust him, or the goons wouldn't have been sent in to see what was going on. Maybe that meant Rosalie and he would be placed under a more careful watch. However, she wouldn't be reined in like that.

Nope.

There'd be no deterring Rosalie from looking for her stolen baby. Austin knew how she felt, but he also knew that her persistence would get her killed the hard way. He couldn't let that happen.

She was right about one thing. He did owe her.

But that was a debt he could never repay.

Still, maybe he could do something to bring his late partner's baby back to her mother's arms.

The guards stepped back. Finally. And as soon as they were out of the doorway, Austin grabbed his shoulder holster and coat from the peg near the door. He still had his backup weapon in the holster in the back waistband of his jeans, but if this little walk to the house went wrong, he wanted all the firepower he could get.

"Come on," Austin told Rosalie and got her moving.

He picked up her Beretta, as well. Or rather, the guard's Beretta. Austin wasn't sure he wanted to know how Rosalie had gotten it from the man.

She glanced back at the guards, who were

now making their way to the barn. Not an ordinary one, either. It had become a modified command post and living quarters to house the guards and all sorts of people who'd been coming and going. Austin had sneaked some photos and jotted down license plate numbers, but he was a long way from piecing this together.

"Why didn't my brother know the FBI had undercover agents working the black market adoptions here?" Rosalie whispered.

"Because the FBI doesn't know I'm here."

Her mouth dropped open, and she looked ready to accuse him of something, but she must have remembered that she'd sneaked in here, too. Of course, he had the training to carry out undercover work.

Rosalie didn't.

But she obviously had some kind of contacts to get her in this place. Austin sure had. Well, one contact, anyway. A former FBI agent who'd helped him create the bogus background and references so Austin would look "legit" to someone running a criminal operation. It had worked, and he'd been hired as head of security at this particular site.

Austin purposely kept their steps slow to give them time to talk, and he looped his arm around her waist so they'd look like the lovers they were pretending to be.

"Who hired you for this job?" he asked.

Rosalie shook her head. "I made all the arrangements through the criminal informant. He said word on the street was the operation was looking for nannies and nurses. I'm an RN. So I had a fake ID made. Created fake work and a computer bio, too."

Austin tried not to groan. Lefty Markham was a piece of slime who'd sell his mother for a quarter.

"The job interview, if you can call it that, was done over the phone," she added. "Along with transportation arrangements. This morning, a truck arrived at an abandoned gas station just off the interstate to pick me up, and the driver made me put on a hood so I couldn't see where he was taking me."

That was standard practice for this operation. So, the fake bio and ID must have fooled the person in charge of hiring her. Still, that didn't mean anyone trusted her.

Nor him.

The camera proved that, and Austin was well aware that he was constantly being watched. Even now.

"You said your daughter was taken eleven months ago?" Austin whispered. He kept them walking at a slow pace toward the house.

Rosalie nodded. "Why? Do you know something about her?"

She sounded hopeful, but Austin would have to crush those hopes right off. "No. I'm here looking for my nephew. He's a newborn, and someone kidnapped him."

Rosalie pulled in a hard breath, and even though it was dark, he thought he might have seen some sympathy in her eyes. "So we can find them both."

"No." He stopped, turned her so she could see that this wasn't up for negotiation. "I'll find them, and you're getting the heck out of here. I don't care how. Pretend you're sick or something. I just want you off the grounds tonight."

She was shaking her head before he even finished. "I can't leave. I have to find my baby." Her voice broke, and he saw the tears shine in her eyes.

Austin huffed. "Look, I know you have no reason to trust me, but you won't be doing your baby any good by getting yourself killed. These men are dangerous, Rosalie, and they'll do whatever it takes to keep this operation secret and profitable."

He could tell by the little sound she made that he hadn't convinced her, so Austin would have to do more than talk. "Then I'll make the arrangements," he added. "But one way or another, you're leaving tonight."

Before she could respond, or argue, the back door to the house creaked open, and the guard staggered onto the porch. Unlike the other two, Austin knew this one. Walter Ludwig. Not very bright but trigger happy.

A bad combination.

Walter had a rifle in his right hand and aimed his left index finger at Rosalie. "She drugged me and stole my gun." And even though he was still staggering, the man pointed the rifle at her.

Austin stepped between them, held up his hands in a calm-down gesture. "Everything's okay," he lied. "It was all just a misunderstanding."

Not the best excuse, but Austin didn't want to say too much. Every word now could be risky.

"She drugged me," the guard repeated, and he came down the steps, closer to where they stood. "And now she's gonna pay for that. Get out of the way, boss."

"Not happening. Just put down the rifle, Walter, and we'll talk about this."

"Don't wanna talk." His words were slurred, and he had to lean against the porch post to steady himself. "I just want her dead real quick."

Austin cursed under his breath. He had to

figure out a way to diffuse this now, or else the other two guards would hear the raised voices and come running. They were already suspicious of Rosalie and him. Which meant the pair just might encourage Walter to commit murder.

"Move away from her!" Walter growled, and despite his unsteady footing, he came off the porch. Charging right toward them.

Austin pushed Rosalie to the side so he could latch on to the rifle and turn it away from her. Walter's finger was on the trigger. Poised and ready to fire.

"If you shoot, a bullet could ricochet and hurt one of the babies," Austin tried again.

His attempt at logic didn't work. Walter was in a rage. Every muscle in his body primed to fight, and it was obvious he wasn't going to listen to reason.

"I'm gonna kill her!" Walter snarled, and when he tried to bring up the rifle to do just that, Austin knew he had no choice.

He bashed the Beretta against the side of Walter's head. It wasn't a hard enough hit to kill the man, but it caused him to drop like a bag of rocks to the ground.

"What's going on?" someone asked, and a moment later, the nanny, Janice Aiken, looked out from the kitchen door. She gasped, pressing her fingers to her mouth.

But that wasn't the only voice that Austin heard.

The barn door opened, and he knew it wouldn't be long before both guards came out to see what was wrong. This had plenty of potential to end in the worst possible way.

"What should we do?" Janice asked. "I'll help."

"She's on our side," Austin explained to Rosalie.

Well, maybe.

He didn't have time for details and especially didn't have time to make sure that he trusted Janice. So far, it appeared the nanny was ready to put an end to the black market baby operation, but he wasn't a hundred percent sure of that. He definitely hadn't counted on trusting her this soon. But one thing he did know: the babies were worth a lot of money, so even if Janice was in on the scheme, she would indeed protect them.

For now, that had to be enough.

Austin turned to Rosalie, took out one of the keys and handed it to her. "It's for the truck. Use it in case something goes wrong. For now, go inside and help Janice get the babies ready to move."

Rosalie gave a shaky nod and hurried into the house with the nanny. They'd barely gotten the back door closed when Austin reeled around and faced the pair of guards who were storming toward them.

"What the hell happened?" one of them demanded.

"Personal dispute. Walter here wanted to sample my lady friend, and I didn't want to share."

Walter moaned, twisting on the soggy ground. "She drugged me."

And despite the moans, that accusation came through crystal clear.

Austin smirked at the man. "I think Walter just had a little too much to drink."

Yeah, it wasn't much of an explanation, but Austin didn't think he could say or do anything at this point that would convince the guards that this was nothing that concerned them.

The guard on the right glanced at Walter. Then, Austin. And finally at the house. "Get the woman out here now so we can talk to her."

That put a hard knot in Austin's stomach. "And then what? You kill her and leave us without a nurse? What happens if one of the babies gets sick, huh?"

The man lifted his shoulder, took aim at Austin. "Nurses are replaceable. And so are you. Drop your weapons."

Oh, man. He really hadn't wanted it to come down to this because the guards likely knew some critical information that would help him find his nephew. And Rosalie's baby. That wouldn't happen if he had to kill all three of them.

Or if they managed to kill him first.

Austin adjusted the grip on his gun so he'd be ready in case the bullets started. He'd have to shoot the one on the right first, dive to the side and hope he got lucky enough to take out the second before the guy got off a shot.

Risky at best.

But his only option now.

Austin brought up his hand, ready to fire, but it was already too late.

The guard pulled the trigger.

Chapter Three

Rosalie and the nanny barreled up the stairs toward the nursery, but the sound of the blast stopped Rosalie in her tracks.

Oh, mercy.

Had the guards killed Austin?

It didn't matter that he was essentially her enemy. She didn't want him shot, especially since he'd been trying to cover for her.

Rosalie hurried into the nursery, running past Janice to get to the window. She braced herself to see a dead Austin lying on the ground, but the only person she saw was Walter. He was crawling back toward the porch. No sign of Austin or the two other guards.

"What's happened?" the nanny asked, and she scooped one of the sleeping newborns into her arms.

Rosalie shook her head just as she heard another shot. It was so loud that it seemed to shake the entire room.

She managed to get a glimpse of Austin. He was still armed, but he was pinned down near some shrubs on the side of the house. The guards had taken up cover behind what was left of the tractor and hay baler.

"We need to get out of here," Janice reminded her.

Yes, they did. But Rosalie watched as Austin had to scramble away from yet another shot. He was doing this to give them a chance to escape, but it could turn into a suicide mission for him.

"Let's go," Janice pressed. She put both of the tiny babies in a single carrier seat and looped the handle over her left arm.

"Is there another gun in the house?" Rosalie asked.

Janice's head jerked up. "There's one on the top of fridge. It's in the way back, so it's hard to see and reach. But you can't be thinking of helping him."

Yes, that's exactly what she was thinking. Rosalie wasn't sure she wanted to trust this woman with the truth about what she was really doing there, but the bottom line was that Austin might be her best bet in finding her daughter. Because it was personal for him, too, since he was on a mission to find his nephew.

Plus, there was the part about his owing her for Eli's death.

It wasn't exactly fair to play the guilt card, but she was many steps past being desperate. She'd do *anything* to find Sadie.

"Here," Rosalie said and pressed the truck keys into the nanny's right hand. Too bad she didn't have a phone to give her, as well, but the guards had taken those from them. "The truck's out front, away from the gunfire. Get the babies out of here."

"But what about you? The boss said we should leave," Janice reminded her.

Rosalie ignored that and got Janice moving. Thankfully, the sound of more shots caused the woman to hurry, and they made their way down the stairs and to the front of the house.

"Drive toward the interstate," Rosalie instructed. "And stop at the first police or fire station you see."

Janice gave a shaky nod and one last look before she raced out the door and to the truck. Rosalie didn't wait to watch her leave. She figured the moment the guards heard the roar of the engine that they'd try to stop the nanny from fleeing with the babies.

That couldn't happen.

Rosalie hadn't been able to protect her own child from being taken, but she could do something about these two. She went to the kitchen, slapped off the lights and stood on her tiptoes so she could search the top of the fridge.

She found the gun.

It didn't take long, just a few seconds, before she heard the truck start. The guards heard it, too, and one of them lifted his head, ready to bolt toward the vehicle.

Austin stopped him.

He fired a shot, sending the man back behind the tractor. But he didn't stay put. The guard and his partner started firing. Nonstop.

All the bullets were aimed at Austin.

Walter kept crawling, coming closer to the house, and Rosalie saw him lift his rifle toward Austin. She wasn't sure Austin would be able even to see the man, and it was a risk she couldn't take.

Rosalie didn't think beyond giving the babies the best possible chance at escape. She opened the kitchen door, and the fridge, as well, so she could use it for cover once she fired.

Walter spotted her right away and pointed the gun at her. However, she pointed her gun right back at him.

And she got off the first shot.

She hadn't aimed for any particular part of him, but the bullet slammed into either his chest or his shoulder, causing him to drop back to the ground.

God, had she just killed a man?

As horrible as that thought was, it would be worse if Walter had managed to shoot Austin, Janice or the babies.

The other guards cursed at her, and both fired into the house. Even over the sound of those shots and her own heartbeat crashing in her ears, she heard Austin.

"Get down!" he yelled.

Rosalie didn't do that. She fired another shot at the guards. Austin did the same, and it kept the men pinned down long enough that they weren't able to stop Janice from escaping. Rosalie caught just a glimpse of the truck taillights as the nanny sped away.

The relief flooded through her.

And the fear.

What if the guards had already managed to call someone to get them out there to the road? And what if they managed to stop the truck? She doubted they would hurt the babies. There was too much money to be made from them.

But they'd kill Janice.

"You're both gonna die!" one of the guards shouted.

The threat had no sooner left his mouth when Austin fired again. Two shots. One for each guard. And both men dropped to the ground.

Everything seemed to freeze. The cold rain.

The echo of those shots. The lifeless guards. Everything except Austin. With his gun still pointed at the guards, he jumped onto the porch and went straight toward her.

"Whoever's on the other end of the cameras will send someone after us," Austin warned her. "We have to move fast."

Rosalie knew he was right, but like the rain and the guards, she felt frozen. Austin helped with that, too. He took her by the arm and ran out of the house with her. Not toward the driveway, where Janice had just driven away. But rather toward another barn that looked ready to collapse under the weight of an old, sagging roof.

"Firing at those guards was stupid," Austin snarled. "You could have been killed."

She wanted to argue, wanted to remind him that he could have been killed, as well, but Austin kept her moving. Running. And when he threw open the barn door, she saw the other truck.

"Where's the nanny?" he asked, shoving her inside the vehicle.

"I told her to drive to a police or fire station."

If he approved of that, he didn't say. Instead, he hotwired the truck, fast, the engine roaring to life, and he slammed on the accelerator. The back tires skidded on the wet, slippery ground, but Austin quickly gained control.

"I'll need to drop you off somewhere." He spared her a glance before those lawman's eyes kept watch around them again. No doubt for anyone following them. "I have something I need to do."

"Something involving this baby farm?"

He didn't answer her right away. "Yeah."

There was a lot of emotion in that one-word response. Rosalie didn't know Austin that well, but she'd been engaged to an FBI agent. Was the sister of one. She knew the personal risks they were willing to take.

"Your cover's been blown," she reminded him.

Well, it had been if any of those guards had survived or if the people behind those cameras had been able to figure out what was going on. Heaven knew who was already on the way out to intercept them.

Austin just shook his head. "I have something important to do. Keep watch," he added, his voice clipped now.

She did. Rosalie kept her gun ready, but that didn't stop the feeling that Austin was withholding something she needed to know.

"There's a safe house about ten miles from here," he explained. "I'll drop you off there and call someone to come and get you. Seth can put you in protective custody."

Because she would now be a target. Rosalie didn't welcome that, but she'd known it was a risk before she'd ever started this.

"Where are you going?" she pressed.

Austin mumbled something she didn't catch. Cursed. Then, he shook his head. "There's a second place. Not too far away. Once I have you safe, I can go there."

It took a moment for that to sink in. "You mean another baby farm?"

"Yeah. It's a lot bigger than this one. Maybe even the command center for the entire operation."

Mercy. This was exactly what she'd been looking for. Despite the ordeal of the shooting and the breakneck speed that Austin was driving, Rosalie could feel a glimmer of hope.

"I haven't been able to get onto the grounds of this second house to access the records," he continued, "but I know there are babies being held for processing. If the guards heard about what just happened here, they'll shut down that place and move the babies."

Austin's gaze slashed to hers for just a second. "My nephew could be there."

"And my daughter. Or at least the records to show me where she was taken. I have—"

"I can't take you with me. It's too dangerous."

Rosalie heard the words, and she knew they were true. But that didn't matter. "I'm going with you. You can't stop me."

That brought on some more profanity. "It's dangerous," he repeated.

"Do you really think I care about that now or that I want you to care about it?" Despite the high speed, she scooted closer to him, so he could hopefully see the determination in her eyes. "Put yourself in my place."

Her voice broke. And the blasted tears came. Tears that wouldn't do Sadie any good, so Rosalie tried to choke them back.

"I have to find my daughter," she managed to say. "And you'd just be wasting time taking me to the safe house. The guards could be moving the babies and records right now. If that happens, we might never find them."

Again, no immediate answer. He just volleyed glances among the road, their surroundings and her, but Rosalie saw the exact moment that he realized she was right.

"You'll stay in the truck," he snapped. "And don't make me regret this."

Rosalie didn't say anything. Didn't want to utter a word that would make him change his mind. She only wanted to get to the house and see if her daughter was there.

Or any babies for that matter.

Yes, Sadie was her priority, but she couldn't bear the thought of any child or parent going through this.

Austin took the next turn off the road. Then, another. Thankfully, he seemed to know exactly where he was going. That would save time, but would it get them there fast enough?

Rosalie remembered the communicator that one of the guards had been wearing when they'd stormed into the cottage and found Austin and her in bed. If the guard had been wearing that during the attack, then someone would have already been alerted to a problem. The people behind this would soon link that problem back to Austin and her.

And Janice.

Rosalie added a quick prayer that the nanny had already made it to safety with the babies. Too bad she didn't have a way to contact Janice, but maybe they could do that soon.

"Thank you," she whispered to Austin.

"Don't," he snapped like a warning. "Because I'm not doing either of us any favors here." He paused and, even in the dim light from the dash, she saw his jaw muscles stir. "They've killed people, Rosalie. And they'll kill again."

That reminder caused her heartbeat to kick up a significant notch, and she thought there was even more that Austin had to say. But he didn't say it.

He just kept driving.

The rain was coming down harder now, the wipers slashing at the fat drops, but it was still hard to see. It got even harder when Austin turned off his headlights and slowed down. Using just the parking lights to guide them, he turned onto another road, drove about a quarter of a mile and then brought the truck to a stop.

He cursed.

"What's wrong?" she asked, but Rosalie was afraid to hear the answer.

"There should be vehicles." Austin got his gun ready, opened the door a fraction and looked around them. He killed the parking lights. Inched closer.

Once her eyes adjusted to the darkness, she saw the silhouette of what appeared to be a large metal barn. Austin was right—no vehicles. No lights, either. The place looked deserted.

He reached over, his hand brushing her leg, and he grabbed a flashlight from the glove compartment. He flicked it on and turned it toward the ground.

That set off another round of profanity.

"There are plenty of tire tracks that have dug into the muddy road," he relayed. "We must have just missed them."

No! It felt as if someone had just clamped a fist around her heart, and Rosalie tried to choke back a sob.

"Maybe they left records." She hoped so, anyway.

Austin inched the truck closer to the building while he kept the flashlight aimed at the ground. He turned it off only when they reached the front of the barn.

The double sliding metal doors were wide-open, and it was pitch-dark inside. If anyone was lurking in there ready to attack, Rosalie couldn't see them.

"Get down," Austin ordered.

She did. Rosalie got onto the floor as Austin drove right into the building.

"Empty," he mumbled.

But then he hit the brakes.

Rosalie lifted her head to try to see what had captured his attention. It appeared to be a white piece of paper nailed to one of the walls.

Austin turned on the flashlight, pointed it toward the paper, and she saw the words scrawled there.

You're a dead man, John Mercer.

"John Mercer," Austin repeated. "That's the name I've been using at the baby farm."

That hardly had time to register in her head when she heard the slight hissing sound.

"Hold on!" Austin shouted. He threw the truck into reverse and slammed his foot on the accelerator.

Just as the wall of fire shot up in front of them.

Chapter Four

Austin held his breath and prayed that he'd get Rosalie away from the building in time.

The truck bolted through the doors, and the moment they were outside, Austin spun the steering wheel to get them on the road. He hit the gas again and got them moving.

Not a second too soon.

Behind them, the building burst into a fireball.

Obviously, someone had put a hefty amount of accelerant inside, and it'd worked. It wouldn't take long for anything left inside to be destroyed.

Hell.

These goons were trying to cover their tracks, and in doing so they might have erased the very information that he needed to find his nephew.

"Call 911," he told Rosalie, tossing her his phone. Austin kept watch around them to make sure they weren't about to be ambushed. The narrow road was lined with trees on both sides, and that meant plenty of places for the shooters to hide. "Tell them we need the fire department and the locals out here. I want this entire area sealed off."

Austin wasn't sure how she managed it because her hands were shaking so hard, but Rosalie made the call. Maybe, just maybe, there might be something left to recover.

"I have to find out if Janice made it to someplace safe," Rosalie said the moment she finished the 911 call. "Oh, God," she added in a mumble. "What if the local county cops are in on this?"

"Don't borrow trouble," Austin reminded her.

He took his phone, scrolled through the numbers, located the number of his partner at the FBI, and gave the cell back to Rosalie. "Text him. Tell him to BOLO Janice Aiken and that she's driving a black truck registered to my undercover alias, John Mercer." Austin rattled off the license plate. "I want him to call me the minute he finds her."

"BOLO," she repeated while she wrote the text. "Be on the lookout."

She'd obviously picked up some cop jargon from Eli or maybe her stepbrother Seth. Austin figured Seth wasn't going to like Rosalie's rogue investigation, and Rosalie wasn't going to like it when Austin called her stepbrother so that Seth could force her to back off. Since she wouldn't listen to him, he had no choice about doing that.

"These baby thieves know you've betrayed them," Rosalie said after she finished the text.

Yeah, they did. The note proved that.

You're a dead man, John Mercer.

And while the idiots behind the baby farms probably didn't know his real identity, it wouldn't be long before they figured out he was FBI. After all, they had countless images of him from those surveillance cameras.

Of Rosalie, too.

"You shouldn't have come here," he insisted. Obviously, he was repeating himself, but Austin hoped she realized just how much danger she was in.

"You came," she pointed out.

Austin tossed her a scowl. The only thing he knew about Rosalie was what Eli had told him. That she was the quiet, shy type who was downright squeamish about his job as a federal agent.

Well, she'd clearly changed *a lot*.

This was no quiet, shy woman next to him. Or maybe Rosalie had just managed to put her squeamishness aside so she could find her daughter. Still, that wouldn't happen if she got herself killed.

"What do we do now?" she asked. "What if

there's no evidence to recover from that building or the baby farm?"

Austin slowed as he approached the junction that would take him back to a main road. "I continue the investigation, and you go home."

She huffed and would have no doubt argued with him about that if the movement hadn't grabbed their attention.

Austin was almost at a full stop at the intersection when someone darted out in front of the truck. He automatically pushed Rosalie down onto the seat, and in the same motion, he took aim at the man.

"Don't shoot!" the man yelled. He had his hands in the air but almost immediately dropped one to his arm. Thanks to the headlights, Austin could see blood on the sleeve of his jacket. "They tried to kill me."

Austin had a fast debate with himself. He could just drive off and call for someone to come and get the guy. After all, despite that injury, this man could be part of this baby farm operation.

And that's why Austin lost that mental debate.

Because if he was indeed part of the operation, then that meant he had answers, and Austin wouldn't get those answers if he allowed him to disappear. Or die.

"Stay down," Austin warned Rosalie.

Did she listen?

No, of course not.

She lifted her head, and Austin nudged her right back down before he lowered his window.

"I need help," the man insisted, walking toward the truck.

"Don't come any closer," Austin warned him, and he took aim at him. "Who are you?"

"Sonny Buckland. I'm a P.I. from Austin."

"Send another text to Sawyer Ryland, my partner at the FBI," Austin told Rosalie. "Have him run this guy's name and ask him to hurry." While she did that, Austin pinned his attention to the man. "Open the sides of your jacket so I can see if you're armed."

"I'm not," he insisted, and he winced when he pulled back the side with the blood. "They took my gun when they found me snooping around the place."

"They?"

"Three armed guards. Big guys. The only reason I managed to escape is because they got a call from someone who told them to get out fast. I ran. That's when one of them shot me."

That meshed with what Austin figured had happened. The person monitoring the cameras at the baby farm had likely made the call to let the guards at this place know there'd been a breach in security.

"How do you know I don't work for those guards?" Austin came right out and asked.

"If you did, you would have already killed me."

True. But that didn't mean Austin would blindly trust this guy. The guards could have left him behind with orders to finish off anyone who got near the place.

Sonny clamped his hand over his injured arm and fired nervy glances all around them. "Stating the obvious here, but it's not safe to hang around. We need to get out of here."

Austin nodded. "You're not going anywhere with us until you convince me you're not working for the baby snatchers."

"I'm not working for them!" Sonny practically yelled. Then, he groaned, a mixture of pain and frustration. "A client hired me to find his missing pregnant friend. I followed some leads that I got from a criminal informant, and it led me to this place."

Rosalie made a soft sound of agreement, and even though Sonny's story meshed with hers about getting the info from a CI, Austin shot them both scowls for inserting themselves into a dangerous investigation. Yeah, he'd done the same thing. And not with authorization, either. But he was a trained agent. Neither of them was.

Of course, Sonny could still be a threat.

"Did you learn who was behind this operation?" Rosalie asked the man. "Did you find any records or anything that could help us locate some missing babies?"

Sonny huffed and made more of those uneasy glances around. He looked on the verge of trying again to press Austin to get him out of there, but maybe he realized the fastest way for that to happen was to give them any info he had.

"I did learn something," Sonny said. Then, paused. "I think a piece of scum named Trevor Yancy is responsible for at least some of the baby kidnappings."

Rosalie sucked in her breath, and her hand went to her mouth. Austin tried to rein in any response, but just like that, his thoughts jerked him back to a bad place, a bad time.

Eli's murder.

Rosalie was no doubt doing the same thing. Because the man Eli and he had been investigating for gunrunning and a whole host of crimes was none other than Trevor Yancy.

"You know Yancy," Sonny said. Not a question, either.

Obviously Austin hadn't done a good job of hiding his reaction. No surprise there. Austin was responsible for the way that investigation had turned out, and it had turned out in the worst possible way.

With Eli shot dead by an unknown assailant.

And Yancy a free man.

If Yancy was indeed involved with the baby farms, then the question was why? Was it just another illegal venture on his part, or was there something even more sinister going on here? Something to do with Rosalie and him?

"What makes you think Yancy's connected to this?" Austin demanded.

Sonny shook his head. "I'll tell you once we're out of here. These men will kill us all if they come back."

Austin couldn't dispute that, and despite his need for the truth, he could no longer keep Rosalie at the center of this possible danger. He was already responsible for Eli's death. Best not to add hers to the nightmares that he stood no chance of ever forgetting.

With a firm grip on his gun, Austin opened his truck door, but before he could get out, Rosalie caught his arm. "You're not going out there."

For a split second Austin was taken aback by her concern. Her touch, too. But just as quickly as she'd touched him, she pulled away her hand. He realized then that her concern wasn't aimed at him but rather their situation. If he got shot, her chances of getting out of there and finding her daughter would decrease big-time.

"I'm only going to frisk him," Austin told her.

He stepped from the truck and did just that. Sonny cooperated, lifting his hands away from his body and wincing in the process.

"No gun, like I said," Sonny explained. "But I've lost some blood."

Yes, he had, and that meant Austin's first stop had to be a hospital, and the nearest one was back in the ranching town of Silver Creek. He could leave Rosalie there, as well, since he knew the sheriff and deputies. He doubted Rosalie would like that, but Austin didn't intend to give her a choice.

"You can ride in the back of the truck." Austin motioned for Sonny to hop in, and the man did. It was freezing cold and wouldn't be a pleasant ride, especially considering his injury, but Austin couldn't risk allowing him in the cab of the truck with Rosalie and him.

"Keep an eye on him," Austin said to her when he got back in.

He checked the road to make sure no one was out there waiting for them, and when Austin didn't see anyone, he got them out of there fast.

"Trevor Yancy," Rosalie mumbled. She turned in the seat so she could nail her attention to Sonny. "Has his name come up in your investigation of the baby farms?"

"No." Austin didn't have to think about that, either. A lot of names had popped up. Potential suspects and kidnap victims. But if he'd seen anything about Yancy related to this, he would have definitely remembered.

"Is it possible…?" Rosalie's breath hitched, and even though they weren't touching, Austin could practically feel her muscles tensing. "Would Yancy have kidnapped my daughter and your nephew because Eli and you had been investigating him?"

Anything was possible when it came to a snake like Yancy.

Anything.

And since that wasn't likely to make Rosalie's breath stop hitching, Austin didn't spell it out for her. Still, this could be the lead that Austin had been searching for. He reached for his phone to have someone bring in Yancy for questioning, but it dinged before he could do that.

"It's a text from FBI Agent Ryland," Rosalie relayed. She still had hold of his phone and stared down at the screen. "He said there's a Sonny Buckland who's a P.I., and he's attached a photo of him." She held it out for Austin to glance at.

The photo was definitely of the same man who was now riding in the bed of the truck. At least Sonny hadn't lied about his identity, but that didn't mean Austin was anywhere close to trusting him.

"Sonny has no criminal record," Rosalie continued to read. She paused though and cleared her throat. "And your partner wants to know what the heck is going on, except he used a lot more profanity than I just did. He also wants you to call him *now*."

She showed him that part of the text, too, though Austin didn't have to see it to know that Sawyer had likely figured out that Austin wasn't on vacation as he'd claimed. Nope. He was on an unauthorized undercover investigation that had just gone to hell in a handbasket.

"I'll call him as soon as I've dropped off both Sonny and you," Austin said more to himself. Rosalie obviously heard it, though.

"I want to go with you to question Yancy or anyone else connected to this," she insisted.

"Yeah, I bet you do, but it's not going to happen. No way will I put you in danger like that."

"I'm already in danger!" she practically shouted, but the fit of temper disappeared as quickly as it'd come. "I need to find my daughter. Eli's daughter," she added, probably because she figured it would touch every raw nerve in his body and soften him up.

He couldn't let it work on him.

His phone vibrated, indicating he had an incoming call, and he saw Sawyer's name on the screen. His partner had obviously meant that part about Austin calling him back now.

Bracing himself for questions he wasn't ready to answer, Austin took his phone, issued another "Keep watch" to Rosalie and answered the call. He didn't put it on speaker, and that was probably the reason Rosalie scooted across the seat— so she could hear.

"Well?" Sawyer said the moment Austin answered.

"I was looking for my missing nephew," Austin settled for saying.

"Yes, and our boss already figured that out. He's not happy, Austin, and he wants you back from your *vacation.*"

"I'll be back soon." He hoped. "For now, I just need your help. I'm en route to the Silver Creek hospital to drop off an injured P.I. who's either a witness or a person of interest in some assorted felonies. I'll be there in about five minutes. Can you make some calls and arrange for him to be guarded?"

Sawyer didn't answer for several snail-crawling moments. "Sure."

"I also need you to have someone secure two crime scenes on the farm road that runs directly east of the town of Silver Creek," Austin added. "Both were baby farms and are owned by a dummy corporation, Real Estate Investments.

There's not much left of them, and there are possible explosives planted around the grounds."

"I'll get someone out there right away," Sawyer assured him. Another pause. "You had a BOLO on a woman driving a black truck registered to your alias?"

"Yeah—"

"A deputy here in Silver Creek just phoned it in. They found her." Sawyer paused again. "It's not good news, Austin. The woman's dead."

Chapter Five

Rosalie's heart went to her knees. She couldn't stop the brutal thoughts and images from going through her head. Images of Janice's frantic escape from the baby farm and the ordeal that had led up to it.

At the time Rosalie had believed that escape was the woman's best chance of surviving.

Obviously, she'd been wrong.

"Oh, God." Rosalie grabbed the phone from Austin and put it on speaker. "What about the babies? Janice had two newborns with her."

"Who is this?" Agent Ryland snapped.

Austin mumbled some profanity and made the final turn toward the hospital. "She's Rosalie McKinnon."

Agent Ryland repeated her name. "She was engaged to Eli." Even though Rosalie didn't know Agent Ryland, the man obviously knew her since it wasn't a question.

"And she's also Seth Calder's stepsister," Austin added. "I ran into her while I was under-cover." He glanced at her, as if he might add more, but then shook his head. "Now, what about the babies?"

"Both are fine. According to the deputy, Janice drove to the sheriff's office, but she was already injured when she got there. She'd been shot."

Rosalie's heart just kept dropping. She was beyond thankful that the babies were okay, but it was terrifying to think of Janice being pursued by these monsters while she was trying to get the newborns to safety.

"The babies are being taken to the hospital," Agent Ryland continued. "Just as a precaution. There's not a scratch on them. And, of course, child protective services will be brought in. Will the woman's killer try to come after the babies?" he came right out and asked.

Rosalie already knew the answer and dreaded hearing it.

"Possibly," Austin said without hesitation.

"I'll get right on it," Ryland answered, also without hesitation, and he ended the call.

"This is all my fault," she whispered.

Austin made a yeah, right sound. "The fault lies with the person who set up the baby farm."

True, but if she hadn't put Janice in a position where she had to escape, the woman might be alive. "If I'd stayed with her and the babies, this might not have happened."

"Yes, it would have, and you'd be dead, too. Those guards wouldn't have wanted any witnesses to get away."

And since both Austin and she were just that—witnesses—then, yes, the men would have tried to shoot her, too. But at least if she'd been there, she might have been able to stop it and Janice might be alive.

Austin drove into the hospital parking lot and came to a stop directly in front of the E.R. doors. Sonny climbed out, not easily, and while still clutching his injured arm, he headed inside.

"Stay close to me," Austin warned her, and as he'd done while they were on the road, he kept watch around them.

The rain had stopped, but the wind took a swipe at her. She was already shivering from the spent adrenaline, and the bitter cold only made it worse.

The moment the E.R. staff saw Sonny, they rushed forward and whisked him away to one of the examination rooms. A security guard wearing a uniform trailed along behind them.

Rosalie looked around, hoping to see the babies and whoever was guarding them, but the E.R. was empty except for a woman sitting at the intake desk.

"I'll need to get some information from you about the patient," the woman said.

But Austin waved her off. "Nothing much we can tell you. We just gave him a ride here."

That wasn't the whole truth, of course, but Austin probably didn't want to get into any details of the investigation with someone who wasn't law enforcement.

"I'll check on the babies," Austin said when Rosalie continued to look around.

He took out his phone, stepped to the far side of the room, but before he could make a call his phone rang. He groaned and showed her the name on the screen.

Seth.

Now it was Rosalie's turn to groan. Agent Ryland had likely called Seth.

"Let me talk to my sister," Seth ordered. Even without the call being on speaker, she had no trouble hearing him.

"I'm fine," Rosalie jumped to say to her brother when Austin handed her the phone.

"You're not fine if you were in the middle of an undercover investigation. Have you lost your mind?"

Probably. Hard to have a sound mind with her baby kidnapped. "I don't expect you to understand why I did what I did."

"Oh, I understand it all right. I want to find

my niece as much as you do, but I don't want my sister dead in the process. Put Austin back on the phone," he ordered, sounding very much like the hardheaded brother that he was.

"How the hell did she manage to get inside an undercover operation, and exactly how close did she come to dying?" Again her brother's voice was so loud that Rosalie didn't need the speaker function to hear him.

Austin's gaze met hers, and she silently pleaded with him not to tell the truth. It was best if she broke the details to Seth after he calmed down. Whenever the heck that might be.

"Rosalie's okay. She was just in the wrong place at the wrong time," Austin said, but he shot her a glare. No doubt because he wasn't happy about the lie or her involvement in any of this.

"From what I'm hearing, you were both at the wrong place. You do know your boss is ticked off about this?"

"Yeah, I heard," Austin mumbled. "Can't be helped."

"We got a lead on the missing babies," Rosalie volunteered since she doubted Austin wanted to continue to listen to this scolding any more than she did.

She moved closer to the phone, and in doing so, her cheek brushed against Austin's. The slight contact stunned her, as if it'd been more than just an accidental touch, and she eased away from him.

Austin's gaze stayed on her, and he cleared his throat. Obviously, he wasn't any more comfortable touching her than she was touching him.

Except it hadn't been just discomfort on her part.

Rosalie felt that trickle of heat. The kind of man-to-woman heat that she couldn't possibly feel when it came to Austin, so she quickly shoved it aside and hoped it didn't come back.

"Trevor Yancy's name came up in connection with the baby farms," Austin told Seth.

"Hell," Seth mumbled.

And that was Rosalie's reaction, too.

Well, it was after she managed to force that *trickle* to take a hike. It was easier to do now that Yancy was in the forefront of her thoughts.

Yancy and his hired gun could be the people responsible for the attack that had left Eli dead, and she wanted the man to have no further connection to her and her family. However, Yancy might have the ultimate connection if he'd been the one to kidnap Sadie.

"I'll deal with Yancy," Austin continued. "And I'll drive Rosalie home as soon as someone arrives to take over for me here at the hospital."

"Don't take her home yet." Seth cursed,

groaned, cursed again. "I'm tied up with a case here in El Paso, so I'm asking you to do me a favor. Protect her. Make sure these goons don't come after her. And, Rosalie, don't you dare say you can take care of yourself."

Since that's exactly what she'd been about to say, Rosalie just stayed quiet and aimed her own glare at the phone. She loved Seth, and he'd been more of a real brother to her than her own three blood-kin ones had been, but she couldn't stop looking for her precious baby.

No amount of warnings from anyone, including Seth or Austin, would stop her.

"Sawyer said these goons killed a woman," Seth went on, talking to Austin now. "And if so, they could come after Rosalie."

That made her feel a little light-headed. She'd considered that, of course, but what she hadn't realized was that if Austin took her to her family's ranch, that she could put all of them in danger, too. Her pregnant sister, Rayanne, was there. Her father, as well, along with her oldest brother's wife and toddler son. She didn't want them caught up in the middle of this dangerous situation.

"I'll get Rosalie to a safe house," Austin assured him, and before either one could give her a say in the matter, they ended the call.

She had to make Austin understand that she

wasn't going into hiding. "I don't want to go to a safe house. I want to find Sadie."

But she was talking to the air because Austin's attention was no longer on her. It was on the lanky dark-haired man who came through the E.R. doors. Rosalie immediately spotted the silver badge clipped to his belt and figured he was carrying a weapon beneath his buckskin coat.

"Agent Duran?" he said, heading their way. "I'm Deputy Gage Ryland. I'm here to guard the man you brought in."

"Ryland," Austin repeated. "You're Sawyer's cousin?"

The deputy nodded, the corner of his mouth lifting a little. "Around here, just about every Ryland has got a badge." The half smile quickly faded. "Tell me about this guy I'll be guarding."

Austin showed the deputy the photo that Sawyer had sent him on his phone. "His name is Sonny Buckland, a P.I. I found him near a baby farm that I'm investigating."

His mouth tightened. "You think he killed the woman with the babies?"

"No." But then Austin huffed and shrugged. "He was with us when that particular shooting happened, but I can't rule out that he's not part of it in some way. In fact, he could have been the one to give the order to have her shot."

The deputy nodded. "Then, I won't let him

out of my sight. We need to catch the SOB who put a bullet in the woman and endangered those babies."

Rosalie couldn't agree more. "How are the babies? Where are they?"

He tipped his head toward a hall off the E.R. "We brought them in through a side entrance. Two other deputies are with them and will escort them to Child Protective Services when the social workers arrive."

That made her breathe a little easier, but her heart was still slamming against her chest.

"My brother's the sheriff," Deputy Ryland continued, "and he's on his way to what's left of the baby farm sites. We'll have a CSI team out there, and the FBI's been called in."

With all that, they might find something.

Correction: they *had* to find something.

"What exactly happened to Janice? How did she die?" she asked. Part of Rosalie didn't want to know the details, especially since she felt responsible, but the other part of her had to know.

"She was shot," the deputy explained. "It appears the bullet went in through the back window of the truck she was driving, and it struck her in the side of the neck. It's a miracle she managed to get away from her attacker. A miracle, too, that the babies weren't hurt."

Just hearing that spelled out caused her

knees to buckle, and if Austin hadn't caught her, Rosalie was afraid she would have fallen. It wasn't just *these* babies who caused her reaction. Though they were the immediate concern. But if the monster behind this had put these two babies at such horrible risk, then her daughter was in the same danger.

Mercy, it hurt too much to think about that. And she'd tried to keep the bad thought aside. Impossible to do that now that she'd dealt with those guards face-to-face. Rosalie knew what they were capable of and how far they'd go to keep their operation under wraps.

Deputy Ryland must have noticed the alarm on her face and probably in every inch of her body because he grumbled something about checking on Sonny, and he stepped away, no doubt so Austin could tend to her.

"Come on," Austin said, taking her by the arm. "I'll get you to that safe house."

Rosalie wanted to stay put, to learn as much as she could from whatever else Sonny might tell them. However, even she couldn't deny that she was shaken to the core and needed a few hours to regroup.

After that, she'd have to get away from Austin. *Protect her,* Seth had told him, and it didn't matter about the bad blood between Austin and her. She figured Austin had no plans to let her out of his sight.

Well, temporarily, anyway.

He'd likely put her in some other agent's protective custody so that he could get on with finding his nephew and putting an end to the baby farms. He'd want to exclude her while doing that.

But that wasn't going to happen.

"How far is this safe house?" she asked.

"Not far. But we'll have to drive around first to make sure we aren't being followed. And it's not a place we want to use for long. It's best if I make arrangements for another place outside the county."

That would put her even farther away from the baby farm. From Janice's killers, too. But it wasn't a trade-off Rosalie wanted since she needed to find answers about Sadie, and sadly, those killers might have those answers. Once they were at this interim safe house, she would somehow have to convince Austin to stay in the area.

That wouldn't be an easy task.

Austin paused when they reached the E.R. doors and looked out. There were no other vehicles near his truck, just the same ones that had been in the parking lot when they'd arrived.

Still, he hurried, and the moment he had her inside, he drove away.

"You okay?" he asked.

"No." Rosalie didn't even try to lie, especially since she was still shaking.

He made a soft sound of agreement. "I'm sorry. I know the shooting must bring back memories of Eli."

"Everything brings back those memories," she mumbled.

"Yes." And that's all he said for several moments. "I know saying I'm sorry won't help, but I am sorry."

Rosalie heard the words. Every one of them. But she couldn't respond. She'd been raised to be polite. To not do anything intentionally to hurt a person's feelings, but there was no way she could let him off the hook.

Eli was dead.

And Austin was partly to blame.

There were probably a lot of details of the investigation she didn't know, but Seth had given her the big picture. Austin and Eli had been undercover investigating an illegal weapons ring, and when a hired gun of the operation had tried to flee, Austin had gone after him.

And in doing so, Austin had essentially blown their covers.

As a result, Eli had been gunned down a few

seconds later by a second hired thug, who then disappeared along with his partner whom Eli had been chasing. All of this had happened just weeks before Eli and she had planned to walk down the aisle. Rosalie hadn't even had a chance to tell Eli that he was going to be a father since she'd learned the news herself only that morning.

As horrible as all those memories were, they gave her something to focus on. Something other than Janice's murder and the danger to all those babies.

Probably because she was still shivering, Austin cranked up the heat and took the road out of town. He didn't go far, less than a mile, before he turned around and went in the opposite direction.

"See anything?" he asked.

Rosalie was about to say no, but she caught something out of the corner of her eye. A vehicle was parked on a side road. No headlights, and it didn't pull out and follow them. However, because of the events of the night, it put her on edge.

"Yeah, I saw it," Austin said, following her gaze to the side mirror. "It could be a spotter, to try to figure out which direction we're going."

And that meant it could be someone connected to the baby farms. "Too bad we just can't stop and question the person inside."

"Not with you in the truck." Austin continued to glance at the vehicle while he turned back toward town. "I'll try another road."

The words had hardly left his mouth when the vehicle pulled out onto the road, following them.

"Get down in the seat," Austin warned her.

Rosalie slid down, but she stayed high enough so she could watch from the side mirror.

Austin handed her his phone. "Call Sawyer. Tell him there's been a change of plans, that I'm taking you to the Silver Creek sheriff's office instead so they can guard you there."

She hated being pawned off, but her mere presence was stopping Austin from going after the person in the vehicle. Rosalie hoped once he dropped her off that Austin would go in pursuit with plenty of backup.

Before she could press Sawyer's number, the phone rang, and she saw a familiar name on the screen.

Deputy Gage Ryland.

Mercy. She prayed something hadn't happened to the babies. Rosalie pushed the answer button so hard that she nearly broke the phone, and she put the call on speaker.

"Are the babies okay?" she jumped to ask.

"Fine," Deputy Ryland answered. "That's not why I'm calling. Is Agent Duran there?"

"I'm here, but I've got someone tailing me. I'm heading to the sheriff's office now."

"Make a detour to the hospital, and I'll have someone take care of the tail."

Austin and she exchanged an uneasy glance. There'd been nothing urgent in the deputy's voice when she'd met him at the hospital, but there was definitely some urgency now.

"I'm with the injured P.I. you brought in," Gage continued, "and I think you should get back down to the hospital fast. We've got a *big* problem."

Chapter Six

That was definitely not what Austin wanted to hear Deputy Gage Ryland say.

We've got a big problem.

Austin already had enough of those. A dead woman. Two destroyed crime scenes. And a whole mess of loose ends he needed to be working on.

Including taking Rosalie to a safe house.

"What's going on?" Austin asked Gage.

"A guy just showed up at the hospital, and he demanded to see the P.I., Sonny Buckland. I told him it'd have to wait, that he was still being stitched up, but before I could send him on his merry way, Sonny came out of the examining room. Armed. He snatched the security guard's gun and aimed it at the guy. Sonny's holding him at gunpoint now."

Of all the problems that Austin had imagined, that wasn't one of them.

Austin shook his head. "And who exactly is the visitor?"

"Trevor Yancy."

Even in the darkness, Austin could see the surprise dart through Rosalie's eyes.

The concern, too.

"I wouldn't have called you," Gage went on, "but this Yancy idiot is egging Sonny on, along with demanding to see Rosalie and you. I'd really rather resolve this without bullets."

So would Austin, especially since the babies might still be nearby.

"I'm on the way," Austin assured Gage, and he turned and headed in the direction of Main Street.

"I want to go with you," Rosalie insisted. "It'll only waste time if you drop me off at the sheriff's office first. And besides, it sounds as if the sheriff and his deputies already have their hands full."

Austin couldn't dispute any of that, but there was another angle to this. "You've already been put in enough danger tonight."

She took hold of his arm, forcing him to make brief eye contact. It was just a glance, but Austin could see the determination written all over her face.

"Trevor might have kidnapped my daughter," she reminded him. "And your nephew. If he did, I want to see his reaction when you ask him about it."

"You're not getting a chance to see his re-action or anything else." Then, Austin huffed. "Sonny's armed, and I don't want you caught in the middle of whatever beef these two morons have against each other."

And it was that beef that Austin was espe-cially eager to learn more about. Sonny had said he'd suspected that Yancy had played a part in at least some of the baby kidnappings, so that might explain why the P.I. would want to hold Yancy at gunpoint.

But why wouldn't Sonny just have Gage ar-rest Yancy?

Something more was going on here, and Aus-tin intended to get to the bottom of it.

Apparently with Rosalie in tow.

Even if he dropped her off at the sheriff's of-fice, there were no guarantees that she'd stay put. Or that she'd be any safer there than she would be with him. She wasn't under arrest, though he was sure he could come up with some kind of charges to force her to stay put or de-clare her a material witness. Still, it would take time to do that, and time wasn't something that was on his side right now.

If Sonny managed to shoot and kill Yancy,

then Austin might never learn the truth about the stolen babies.

Cursing his situation and this whole blasted mess, Austin drove toward the hospital.

"Thank you again," Rosalie said when she obviously realized where they were going. She also released a long breath, one that sounded as if she'd been holding it for a while.

Austin darn sure didn't say *You're welcome* because he figured there were too many things that could go wrong with this situation.

Especially since both Sonny and Yancy were suspects.

Even if Gage hadn't told him about the trouble going on, Austin would have known something was wrong the moment that he pulled to a stop by the E.R. Several medics and nurses were outside, huddled together against the bitter cold, and they were out there because Gage had almost certainly evacuated the immediate area.

Austin didn't have a badge to flash. It was too risky to carry one while undercover, but no one questioned him when he identified himself as a federal agent and went back into the E.R. He spotted Gage immediately, his gun drawn, and every part of his body on alert.

"Stay here," Austin warned Rosalie, and with his own gun drawn, he went into the hall to join Gage.

There, in the examining room, he saw the tall, heavily muscled man with blond hair.

Yancy.

He was backed into a corner. Literally. He had his hands lifted in the air. Sonny was in the opposite corner, the examining bed between them, and he did indeed have a gun pointed right at Yancy.

Despite the raised hands, Yancy looked calm, wearing an expression more suited for a social visit than a crime in progress. However, Sonny's face was beaded with sweat, and the fresh stitches on his arm weren't even bandaged. Judging from the way the supplies and equipment had been scattered around the room, the medical staff had left in a hurry.

It'd been over a year and a half since Austin had seen Yancy, but the man hadn't changed much. He still wore a pricey suit that probably cost more than Austin made in a month, and he still had that cocky expression that Austin wished he could knock off his face.

Despite the fancy clothes, Yancy was nothing but a rich punk.

"Austin," Yancy greeted, and the corner of his mouth lifted into a dry smile. "How kind of you to come to this little get-together."

Austin ignored his sarcasm and the man himself and instead turned to Sonny. "Put down that gun now, and then you can tell me what the hell this nonsense is all about."

"It's about *him,*" Sonny snarled with his gaze still staked to Yancy. Sonny's hand was shaking, and he was grimacing as if in pain. Not good. Since his shaking finger was also on the trigger. "Yancy came here to set me up."

Austin glanced at Rosalie to make sure she was staying put. She was. "Set you up how?" he asked Sonny.

But Sonny didn't jump to answer, and Yancy's renewed smile made Austin even more uneasy.

"I used to work for Yancy," Sonny finally said. "I was his top security man, and when I discovered some things that didn't mesh, he fired me."

Yancy dismissed that with a carefree shrug. "He violated my privacy by poking his nose where it didn't belong. And he found nothing illegal. Only some personal emails that he misinterpreted."

"Oh, I found something all right," Sonny argued. His gaze slashed to Austin. "But the emails disappeared. That's why I went to the baby farm, looking for proof, and I'm sure it was Yancy who gave the order to have me shot because I was close to finding out that he'd kidnapped all those kids."

Austin heard Rosalie make a sound of surprise. She obviously hadn't missed what Sonny had just said, and almost immediately Austin heard her footsteps, heading straight toward them.

Oh, man.

Austin didn't even bother to tell her to stay back. She wouldn't. Not when she thought she could learn something about her missing baby.

However, he did try to keep himself between her and the gun Sonny was holding. Sonny didn't seem to want to hurt Rosalie, but Austin wouldn't take the risk of a stray bullet coming her way.

"All lies," Yancy said without a shred of guilt in his voice.

"All truth!" Sonny practically yelled.

"Settle down," Austin warned him, and both Gage and he moved closer to Sonny in case they had to go after that gun Sonny was still holding.

"Did you kidnap my daughter?" Rosalie came out and asked Yancy despite his denial just moments earlier.

"Of course not. If I were looking for some way to get back at your late fiancé and Austin for their witch hunt of an investigation, I would have gone after them, not your little girl."

His tone was so placating that Rosalie took a step toward him, as if she might try to force the info from him, but Austin hooked his arm around her and held her back.

Since he figured Yancy would just continue to deny any wrongdoing, Austin went with a different approach. "If you're innocent, why come here to the hospital?" he asked Yancy. "And how the heck did you even know you'd find your former employee here?"

Another shrug from Yancy. "I had my people watching Sonny. A precaution since he'd threatened to get even with me. They followed him to the place that he's calling a baby farm. My men had no idea what it was, of course—"

"You're lying," Sonny snapped. "You knew exactly what it was because the address was in one of those emails I found."

"Ah, the emails that don't exist." Yancy made things a thousand times worse by adding a smile.

Sonny would have gone after him, too, if Austin hadn't stopped him. Thankfully, Gage moved in to protect Rosalie so that Austin could concentrate on diffusing this dangerous situation. He took full advantage of Sonny's pain and shaky hand to knock the gun away from him. Sonny tried to go after it again, but Austin pinned him against the wall.

"You know the deputy here has to arrest you,"

Austin reminded Sonny. "So, don't do anything else stupid to make it worse."

That last part seemed to do the trick because Sonny stilled. Well, his body did, anyway, but he glared first at Yancy and then at Austin. "You're arresting the wrong man. You should be putting that snake behind bars." And he tipped his head to Yancy.

"I'll gladly arrest him, too, if you have any proof that he's connected to the baby farms."

"No proof," Yancy insisted. "And there won't be because I haven't done anything wrong. Well, not recently, anyway. And nothing that I'd confess to doing."

Yancy smirked again.

Mercy, maybe Austin should have let Sonny hang on to that gun. That wasn't exactly a legal brand of justice, but justice might be served in the end if somebody wiped that smirk off Yancy's face.

"If your men followed Sonny as you said," Rosalie continued, talking to Yancy, "then they likely know who killed the woman who escaped."

For the first time since this whole conversation had started, Yancy looked a little bewildered. Of course, that could be faked.

"They didn't see anyone get killed," Yancy insisted. "If they had, they would have reported it to me, and I would have called the cops like any responsible citizen."

"Right," Austin mumbled, slinging some of that attitude right back at Yancy.

"Right," the man repeated. "Make me out to be the bad guy here if you want, but you'll want to press Sonny for more info about the lie he just told about those emails. I'm sure you've already considered he said that to cover his own butt, that he's the one who's involved with the baby farm. It would explain why he was really out there tonight."

Sonny made a sound of outrage. "I was out there looking for proof of your connection," he repeated.

"And you found nothing." Yancy gave him a flat look before turning his attention back to Austin. "I've been doing some digging of my own because I figured Sonny would try to frame me."

"What'd you find?" Austin demanded when Yancy didn't continue.

"You'll want to check on a past acquaintance of Sonny's. A woman named Vickie Cravens."

Sonny cursed. "Don't you dare drag her into this."

Now Yancy lost some of that cool composure. His eyes narrowed, and his teeth came together for a moment. "You started this game by dragging me into it. If you play with fire, then don't expect to stay alive for very long."

"Who's Vickie Cravens?" Rosalie asked.

"Sonny's former lover," Yancy supplied. He put back on the coat that he'd been holding. "She's worked as a nanny from time to time, and I suspect she's working for the baby farms. Maybe even helping him run them."

"She wouldn't have done anything like this," Sonny insisted.

While buttoning his coat, Yancy started out of the room. "Do your job," he said to Austin. "And you'll find Vickie isn't as innocent as Sonny would like her to be." His mouth bent into another of those nails-on-a-chalkboard smiles before he strolled away.

"Vickie's innocent," Sonny muttered. He no longer looked like the man who'd just challenged Yancy with a gun. He sank down onto the edge of the examining table. "It's Yancy who's behind this."

Austin got right in Sonny's face. "And if he is, I'll be the one to find the evidence. No more grabbing guns from guards—"

"I thought he came here to kill me. I needed that gun to defend myself."

Sonny sounded convincing enough, but Austin's mood was well past the stage of just being bad, so he didn't give him any benefit of the doubt.

"Just stay away from this investigation," he warned Sonny. Austin glanced at Rosalie. "You, too. You're not going to try to question Vickie Cravens."

She stared at him, and he could see not just the weariness in her eyes but also the frustration. Vickie could have info about Rosalie's missing baby, but if so, it was info Austin would get without her.

"You can finish up here?" Austin asked Gage.

Gage nodded. "I gotta arrest him for wielding that gun, but if I don't have anything else to charge him with, then I figure he'll be out by morning after he makes bail."

It was a reminder that if Sonny was indeed guilty of the baby kidnappings, then Austin had to find something fast to keep him behind bars. Of course, *fast* couldn't start to happen until he got Rosalie to a safe house.

Austin thanked Gage and got Rosalie moving toward the exit. Even if this incident hadn't just happened, he would have still made sure it was safe to step outside, but he took a second and third look since Yancy might still be out there. Or the person who'd tried to follow them.

"You okay?" he asked Rosalie when she pulled in a long breath.

"No." Since she didn't look steady on her feet, Austin looped his arm around her waist. Her gaze fired to his as if she might object over the close contact, but she only gave a weary sigh.

"Yeah," he mumbled. He knew exactly what that meant. The danger had created a strange partnership that neither of them had seen coming.

Austin was about to hurry them to his truck when his phone rang, and he saw Sawyer's name on the screen. Maybe, just maybe, his partner had found out something so Austin could make an arrest.

"Please tell me you have good news," Austin greeted Sawyer, and he eased Rosalie away from the doors and back into the waiting room.

"Nowhere near it," Sawyer answered.

Austin groaned. "What went wrong now?"

"You did. Just heard something that you're not gonna like. Trevor Yancy sent a boatload of proof about your unauthorized investigation to the deputy director."

Oh, hell. "I'll be there ASAP to clear things up."

"I think it'll take more than talking to do that," Sawyer added. "Because the boss wants your badge *now*."

Chapter Seven

Rosalie stared at the sterile white ceiling of the safe house. Again. She'd been doing a lot of that since Austin and she had arrived about eight hours earlier. Hard to sleep in a strange bed with so many things unsettled both in her mind and with her botched investigation.

Now she had to deal with the danger.

And the fear that she wasn't any closer to finding Sadie than she had been nearly a year ago when someone had kidnapped her.

It was morning now, the sun creating slivers of light through the blinds, but she didn't get up. She didn't have enough energy to force herself to move. Plus, she didn't hear Austin stirring, something that she would have been able to do in the small two-bedroom house.

The place was literally in the middle of a pasture, miles from town. No traffic, no other sounds, so that earlier she'd had no trouble hearing Austin make multiple calls and pace over the bare hardwood floors.

He was just as troubled as she was.

Maybe more, if that were possible. Because from what she'd heard, he hadn't managed to keep his badge. Still, he'd brought her to the safe house and had kept her in his unofficial protective custody.

For now, anyway.

He was probably eager to give that particular duty to someone else so he could continue with the investigation and soothe things over with his boss. Losing his badge would cut him to the core.

That got her moving from the bed. She had to make arrangements for her own security and work out how to continue the investigation while still staying safe. She'd gotten so close before those monsters had destroyed the evidence and killed Janice, and she needed to find another way to get close again.

Maybe Vickie Cravens was the key.

Austin had already made a call about the woman. One of many calls he'd made on the drive to the safe house, and since he was no longer officially an FBI agent, he hadn't been able to request an FBI background check on her.

Still, Sawyer had run one, and he'd gotten Vickie's phone number and address for Austin, but she hadn't answered when Austin had tried to contact her. Austin had left her a message to call him, that he could help her. Rosalie had memorized the number and would try to call Vickie herself as soon as she was someplace safe.

If a safe place existed, that is.

Since she didn't want to go to her family's ranch and bring the danger there, she had to bite the bullet and call her brother Seth. Yes, he'd likely chew her out again for her undercover attempt, but it was better than the alternative of begging Austin to let her tag along with him.

Not that Austin would let her, anyway.

In his eyes, she was the worst kind of trouble and could interfere with his own investigation.

Heck, he probably even blamed her for losing his badge. After all, if she hadn't gone to that baby farm and essentially blown his cover, he might have been able to find the evidence to stop this operation in its tracks. She seriously doubted his boss would have fired him if he'd managed to unravel one of the highest-profile cases in the state.

Rosalie used the small adjoining bathroom to wash up, and she changed into jeans and a gray sweater that she found in the closet. Obviously, things left by the FBI since there were a variety of sizes and clothing items, and it made her wonder how many other women had stayed here while trying to outrun danger.

She, on the other hand, wouldn't try to outrun it if it meant finding Sadie.

Rosalie kept her footsteps light so that she wouldn't wake up Austin but then really wasn't surprised to find him already at the kitchen table, sipping coffee and reading something on his laptop.

He looked about as rested as Rosalie felt— which wasn't very rested at all. His hair was mussed and too long to be regulation length. There probably hadn't been many opportunities for a haircut while he'd been undercover. Like her, he'd changed his clothes and was wearing jeans and a black T-shirt that hugged his chest in all the right places.

She mentally groaned.

No way should she have noticed something like that. And that was yet another good reason to put some distance between them.

"What's wrong?" Austin asked.

Obviously, he'd seen something alarming in her expression. Rosalie was glad he wasn't a mind reader because there was no way she wanted him to know that momentary lapse she'd just had about him.

"Any news?" she asked, helping herself to some coffee while also avoiding his question.

He nodded. "All bad. Want to hear it, anyway?"

Now Rosalie groaned for real, and since she figured she might need to sit for this, she sank down at the table across from him.

"Sonny's already out of jail," he started. "And Yancy doesn't want charges pressed against Sonny. Of course, Gage can still charge him with reckless endangerment, but since Sonny doesn't have a record, I doubt he'll get any jail time."

Rosalie shook her head. "Why wouldn't Yancy want charges pressed against Sonny? Sonny pulled a gun on him."

"Who knows? Maybe because he wants Sonny out of there. That way, if something else goes wrong, Yancy can say that Sonny did it." Austin paused. "And maybe it'd be the truth. Just because he was shot, it doesn't mean I trust Sonny. In fact, that wound could have been self-inflicted so we would trust him. He could have done it so he could figure out how much we learned about the baby farms."

Hearing that aloud sent a chill through her, but she'd had the same reaction to Yancy. It sickened her to think a monster like that might have been the one to take Sadie.

"Still no answer from Vickie Cravens," Austin went on, obviously continuing with that bad news. "Sawyer had a local cop go to her place to do a welfare check, but she wasn't home. There's also no sign of the person who tried to follow us last night or the guards who escaped from the second baby farm."

Maybe because they were all long gone. Both a relief and a scary thought. If they had fled, then they wouldn't be around to try to kill Austin and her. But if they were gone, so was any info they could have given her about who was behind the operation.

"I guess the CSI didn't find anything at the two baby farm sites?" she asked.

"Nothing. They'll keep looking, of course."

Yes, but she was betting the guards had destroyed anything that could prove helpful. "This isn't just a cottage industry," she said, thinking out loud. "The person doing this has money and is well-organized."

"Maybe well-hidden, too." Austin cursed, shoved his hand through his hair and stood. Pacing, again. "I figure this is a pyramid operation. One top dog with lots of sites. Each site operates independently of the others, so if one goes down, it doesn't take the others down with it."

Rosalie swallowed hard. "Then it might be impossible to find the person who took the babies."

"Hard, yes. Impossible, no. I'm not giving up on finding my nephew."

"Even though it cost you your badge?" she asked.

A muscle flickered in his jaw. "I won't stop, no matter what the cost." He sat in the chair next to her and stared straight into her eyes. "But you'll have to. You can't put yourself in the line of fire like this."

Rosalie considered just lying. Telling him what he wanted to hear, that she'd go home and wait for someone else to find her baby. But she was tired of waiting. She'd been the good girl too long, listening to various lawmen who had told her to let them do their jobs.

Well, they hadn't done their jobs.

They hadn't found Sadie.

"I can't stop," she told him. "But it's not your problem."

"To hell it's not. I can't let you go out there and get yourself killed."

"It's not your responsibly to keep me safe."

The flat look he gave her said differently.

Oh, no. They weren't about to go there with this conversation.

"You don't owe me because of Eli," she insisted.

"That wasn't what you said at the baby farm," he reminded her.

"I was desperate, and I blackmailed you, but now I'm letting you off the hook. Besides, you've got enough on your plate." She paused. "How much work will it take you just to get your badge back?"

Austin turned, ready to bolt out of the chair, and she saw the pain this was causing him.

"For what it's worth, I'm sorry," she added. "Eli always said you were married to the badge."

"Yeah." And a moment later, Austin repeated it. "The only thing I've ever wanted to be was an FBI agent. But my sister is blood. So is her son. I have to get Nathan back home before Christmas."

Rosalie nodded, swallowed the lump in her throat because that was her wish, too, for her own baby. "When was Nathan kidnapped?"

"Right after he was born nearly four months ago. My sister had a C-section, and she had some problems with blood loss right afterward. She nearly died, so no one got around to taking pictures of the baby. He was stolen just a few hours later. Someone had tampered with the security cameras and jammed the tracking chip used in the hospital bracelets."

Oh, God. His story brought her own painful

memories to the surface. Not that they were ever far from her mind.

At least she had a photo of Sadie, but her sweet baby had been taken much the same way. A very precise, organized crime since the tracking chip in Sadie's bracelet had been jammed, as well, by placing several Wi-Fi scramblers throughout the hospital. If that hadn't been done, the chip in the bracelet would have triggered the security alarm when the kidnapper stepped outside the hospital with her. As it was, it'd taken the kidnapper less than five minutes to get in and out.

It sickened her to think of how many times that same crime had been committed since the start of these baby farms.

"If you don't know what your nephew looks like, then how will you know if you find him?" Rosalie asked.

Austin seemed to be in such deep thought that it took him a moment to answer her. "According to the nurse who assisted with the delivery, Nathan has a large strawberry-shaped birthmark on his left leg."

That would help, but only if they got a close look at the baby.

"I'm guessing your sister already put this info out there, in case someone adopted a baby with a birthmark like that?" Rosalie pressed.

"Of course." He stared at her. "And no one came forward. I think that probably means that the person who adopted him or bought him knew they were doing something illegal."

Yes. She'd come to the same conclusion. "We don't even know how many babies are missing. From everything I've learned about this operation, they kidnap illegals and homeless girls and force them into surrogacy. They kidnap pregnant women, too, and they steal babies."

"And they murder the women," Austin reminded her. His gaze came to hers again. "That's why you have to back away from this. You can't be a mother to Sadie if you're dead."

Rosalie cursed the blasted tears that watered her eyes. She'd cried an ocean of tears over this, and the crying jags only drained her. They didn't help. And that's why she tried to blink them back.

As she did most other times, she failed.

Austin cursed again, clearly not any happier about the tears than she was, and Rosalie figured it was a good time to go back into the bedroom and get control of herself. She didn't make it far.

Still cursing, Austin reached out, snagged her by the shoulder and hauled her to him. He wasn't gentle. Not at first, anyway. Rosalie could practically feel the frustration in the corded muscles of his arms. But then his grip around her relaxed.

"I'm sorry this happened to you." His voice was gentle, too. Almost a whisper. And even though Rosalie figured that being in his arms was a very bad idea, she just didn't have the strength to push him away.

Austin made a soft shh-ing sound and eased her deeper into his arms. Until she was pressed against him. Even with the tears and her heart shattering, she felt his body. Heard the quick rhythm of his breath.

Felt it, too.

When his chest rose against her breasts.

Just as when she had spotted him at the table with his bedroom hair and eye-catching jeans, the trickle of heat went through her. A bad kind of heat that she didn't want to feel for him. But did, anyway.

Rosalie pulled in her breath, taking in his scent with it, and she got a feeling of a different sort. Her heart raced, slamming against him.

And he noticed, all right.

Heck, maybe she was giving off some kind of weird vibe because Austin pulled back, his gaze meeting hers. His left eyebrow lifted a fraction. Rosalie figured what he was silently asking— was she actually attracted to him?—but it was a question she had zero intentions of answering.

His grip melted off her, and Rosalie stepped back, but his gaze stayed on her mouth. She was well aware of this because her attention stayed on his eyes.

Bedroom eyes, too.

Oh, mercy.

She was in trouble here.

"You've been under a lot of stress," Austin mumbled, as if that explained everything going on between them right now.

Yes, it was a nightmarish time for her, but Rosalie doubted stress could cause this warmth that she was feeling in just about every part of her body. Still, she nodded, accepting the out he'd just given her. She needed to take that *out* a little further though and get the heck out of there and away from Austin.

"You plan to call Seth now?" Austin asked.

Had he read her mind about that, too?

Of course, maybe it hadn't taken any mind-reading powers. She didn't exactly have a lot of options here.

Rosalie nodded and was about to ask if she could use his phone, but it buzzed before she could do that. Since they'd had only bad news all morning, she tried to brace herself for more but prayed for a better outcome.

"It's Vickie," Austin said, glancing at the screen, and he hit the button to put the call on speaker.

"Agent Duran?" the woman immediately said, but she didn't wait for him to answer. "I need to talk to you *now*. Get here to my place as fast as you can. And hurry. They're coming to kill us."

Vickie hung up but not before Rosalie heard a sound on the other end of the line that sliced right through her.

A crying baby.

Chapter Eight

"You don't have time to ditch me," Rosalie repeated. "We have to get to Vickie and stop her and that baby from being hurt."

She'd been saying variations of that same thing during the entire half-hour drive from the safe house to Vickie's house. Austin figured she was right, but still he couldn't risk taking Rosalie into yet another dangerous situation.

That's why he'd called for backup from the San Antonio cops.

Once Austin arrived at Vickie's place, he could hand Rosalie off to the officers and then find out what the heck was going on. Maybe it wasn't too late to help Vickie and get her and the baby out of harm's way.

Of course, *They're coming to kill us* wasn't the kind of thing someone said unless the person was already in harm's way. If he couldn't get to her in time, maybe SAPD could.

Austin pushed the accelerator as hard as it

was safe to do, speeding toward Vickie's house on the outskirts of San Antonio. He also kept watch around them in case the gunmen were using this as some kind of ruse to draw Rosalie and him out into the open again. Rosalie kept watch, as well, her gaze firing all around them while she kept a white-knuckle grip on the armrest.

"The baby could be Sadie," she mumbled.

Yeah, she'd been repeating a version of that, too, since Vickie's call.

"Don't get your hopes up," he said, doing some repeating of his own. There were likely dozens of babies connected to this operation, and the odds were slim that it was Rosalie's daughter.

"Hope is all I have."

Her voice was small and shaky. Barely a whisper. However, Austin heard every drop of the raw emotion in it, and he knew it was going to be a bear to keep her out of this situation. He understood her need to see if this was Sadie, but at the moment he had an even greater need to keep her safe. Then, he could rescue Vickie and the crying baby.

His phone buzzed, and without taking his attention off the road, Austin answered it.

"I'm Detective Hernandez, SAPD," the man

said. "We're at Vickie Cravens's house now, but she's not here."

Rosalie made a sharp sound of concern, mimicking the way that Austin felt. "She could be hiding inside." Austin hoped. Hiding and unharmed.

"We looked," the detective explained. "Her back door was wide-open so I went in and checked every room. She's not here."

Austin hated he had to ask his next question. "Any sign of foul play?" And he held his breath, waiting for the answer.

"Not really, but her purse and car are here, and there's a can of baby formula opened on the kitchen counter. Looks like she left in a hurry."

Or was taken in a hurry. Austin wasn't sure where Vickie had been when she'd made that frantic call to him. It was possible she'd been somewhere else and heading to her house and that's why she'd told him to go there. If she'd seen any signs that it wasn't safe to go inside, she could have escaped. Or maybe the escape had happened after the danger was right on her. Either way, he refused to believe, yet, that the worst had happened.

"Maybe she has two vehicles," Austin suggested. "And she could have used the second one to get away."

"She only has one car registered to her,"

Detective Hernandez explained. "The houses out here are pretty far apart, but we'll canvass the area and talk to her neighbors. She might be with one of them or may have borrowed a car."

Maybe. But as determined as these baby farm guards were, Austin had to admit to himself that they would have already gone after her no matter where she'd tried to flee.

If Vickie had told the truth, that is.

After everything that Rosalie and he had been through in the past twenty-four hours, Austin wasn't about to trust anyone completely. However, he had to do whatever it took to get the baby to safety.

"I'll be there in about five minutes," Austin told the detective.

"Vickie could have gotten away," Rosalie concluded when Austin ended the call. "She seemed to have had some kind of warning, a long enough one to call you."

Yeah. She'd said they were coming to kill her, not that they were already there. Since they'd had enough bad news, Austin decided to hold on to that as a positive sign. Even if Vickie had had only a couple of minutes' head start, it might have been enough for her to escape and hide from her would-be attackers.

But where the heck was she now?

Following the instructions on his GPS, Austin

took the final turn toward Vickie's house. Technically, it was inside the city limits, but it was still fairly rural with the thick trees and narrow road leading to the pastoral-sounding neighborhood of Eden Waters.

He was about to repeat his warning to Rosalie that she couldn't be part of this. The warning died on his lips, however, when he saw the auburn-haired woman. She was partly concealed behind a winter-bare oak tree, and she had something clutched in her arms.

"Vickie," Rosalie and he said in unison.

Austin hit his brakes, pulling his truck to the side of the road, and drew his gun. He also had to catch hold of Rosalie's arm to keep her from bolting.

"She looks terrified," Rosalie insisted.

"And looks can be deceiving," Austin insisted right back. "Plus, this could be some kind of a trap."

But if it was, then it was a darn good one. The woman's gaze met his, and even from the twenty-yard or so distance that separated them, Austin was pretty sure he could see the fear in her eyes.

"We have to protect that baby." Rosalie shook off his grip, and she would have no doubt bolted again if Austin hadn't stopped her.

"Wait here," he ordered, and he made sure

that's exactly what it was. *An order.* Austin handed Rosalie his phone. "Call Detective Hernandez and tell him where we are. I want him here now so he can guard you."

Of course, Austin would still have to keep an eye on Rosalie to make sure she stayed put and that the guards didn't use this opportunity to sneak up on them.

"There's a gun in the glove compartment," he added and gave Rosalie one last glare of warning before he opened his truck door. "I'm Agent Duran," he called out to the woman.

As with the fear he'd seen earlier, he thought maybe now there was some relief. Still clutching the bundle in her arms, she started running toward them. "I'm Vickie Cravens."

"Get down," Austin told Rosalie.

He didn't look back to make sure she did it. He kept his attention nailed to the woman and the area around her. Vickie was doing the same, her gaze darting all around as she made her way to him.

"We have to get out of here," Vickie insisted. "I got a call, and they're on the way."

"Who's on the way?" Austin demanded, and he moved in front of her to block her from getting into the truck.

Vickie's breath was gusting, and she frantically shook her head. "No time to explain now."

Austin would have argued that, but the sound stopped him cold. The baby cried, squirming beneath the blanket, and he knew that he couldn't just stand there and wait for something else bad to happen.

He cursed the fact that Rosalie was in the truck. Cursed also because he had put her right back in the middle of possible danger. He hoped it didn't turn out to be the same kind of mistake he'd made with Eli.

Austin checked as best he could to make sure Vickie wasn't armed, and he helped her onto the seat between Rosalie and him. Thankfully, Rosalie had taken the .38 out of the glove compartment, but Austin prayed neither of them had to use a weapon, especially not in such close quarters.

He spotted the cop car coming up behind them. Hernandez, no doubt. "Call him," Austin said to Rosalie. "Tell him to follow us."

Though her hands were still shaking, Rosalie managed to do that.

"We can't go to SAPD," Vickie quickly said, fumbling to put on her seat belt. "I'm not sure I can trust them. I'm not sure I can trust *you*," she added, volleying glances at both Rosalie and him.

"Then why'd you return my call and ask for help?" Austin pressed.

Vickie choked back a hoarse sob. "Because someone said I could trust you. A friend."

"Sonny?" Rosalie asked. She leaned closer to Vickie, obviously trying to get a look at the baby in the blanket.

"No. Not Sonny. Someone who works as a criminal informant." Vickie didn't hesitate, either. "Why, does Sonny have something to do with this?"

The question was right for someone who was innocent. Her seemingly surprised reaction, too, but again, Austin knew this sort of thing could be faked.

Still, it was best to get answers someplace safer.

He drove off, heading toward Sweetwater Springs. Rosalie wasn't going to like the fact he was taking her back home, but one of her brothers was the sheriff there, and Austin wanted some help that didn't involve the FBI.

"I need to know if the baby is my daughter," Rosalie said.

"No." Again, Vickie didn't hesitate, but she did look puzzled by the question. "It's a boy. Why? Did someone take your baby?"

She nodded, swallowed hard. "Do you know anything about a missing baby girl? She'd be eleven months old." Rosalie took hold of the woman's arm, turning her so that Vickie was facing her. "Do you know where my daughter is?"

"No. I'm sorry. I didn't see any records, not for your baby or anyone else. I just got a few emails and phone calls. Mostly from the fake adoption agency and then a few from the couple who was supposed to adopt this baby."

That was a start. Records weren't the only thing that could help Rosalie and him. Once they had the name of the person responsible, then they could force him or her to talk.

Of course, Vickie could be that person.

And it could be his nephew she had in her arms.

Austin couldn't see much of the child because of the way Vickie had him clutched against her, but he could see the baby's wispy brown hair. Maybe the color of his nephew's hair. He just didn't know.

Heck, he didn't even know if this baby was four months old, the right age for his sister's missing son.

"Why do you have this child?" Austin demanded.

Vickie gave another hoarse sob. "I didn't know the operation was illegal. I swear, I didn't. I just needed a job, and I'd done work as a nanny. That's why I wasn't suspicious when this nanny agency contacted me out of the blue and asked if I'd take a temporary position to care for a newborn."

"I want the name of the agency and the person who contacted you," Austin insisted.

"It's fake. I figured that out when I got suspicious and tried to call them, but the number wasn't working. Neither was the email they'd used to contact me. I was only supposed to keep the baby for a couple of days, until his adoptive parents picked him up, but the days turned to weeks. Someone from the agency kept calling, saying it wouldn't be much longer."

So, something had obviously gone wrong. But if this baby was connected to the pair of now-destroyed baby farms, then why hadn't the person in charge come and taken the child? A healthy baby boy would have fetched a good price for a black market adoption.

"I still want the name of the agency. The adoptive parents' names, too," Austin continued. Though those were probably fake, as well, if the agency had been. "You'll also give me a detailed statement of everything that went on from the moment this agency contacted you."

Vickie nodded, moaned softly. At least Austin thought she'd moaned, but he realized Rosalie had made that sound. She was staring down at the baby, but he could see the pain all over her face. This wasn't her child. Her baby was still out there somewhere, and it was shattering her heart.

Just as it was doing to Austin's own sister.

"I called Sonny," Vickie went on before Austin could ask more about the baby in her arms. "I told him something suspicious was going on. He said he'd check things out for me."

"Is that why he was at the baby farm?" Rosalie asked.

Vickie's eyes widened. "A baby farm? God, how many babies were taken?"

"We're not sure," Austin answered. It was the truth, but he also didn't want to give Vickie too many details. Even if she was innocent, she might warn Sonny. Or she might even be connected to Yancy. "When did you call Sonny?"

"Last night."

If that was true, then Sonny had found the place darn fast. Either that meant Sonny had gotten lucky or he'd known where to look. The uneasy glance Rosalie gave him let Austin know that she'd come to the same conclusion. Soon, very soon, he needed to question Sonny again because the man hadn't been the one to bring up Vickie's name back at the hospital.

Yancy had.

Maybe Sonny hadn't wanted to implicate Vickie in this, and that could have been the very reason Yancy had told Austin about the woman. Either way, Sonny might be able to give them answers.

"How old is that baby?" Austin asked. It was hard to do with his thoughts scattered in a dozen different directions, but he tried to keep watch around them. Tried to keep his emotions in check, too.

"Four months. I've had him with me since he was just a couple of days old."

The age was right, after all. Austin had to force himself to release the breath he was holding. He also had to tamp down the hope he felt rising in his chest.

Rosalie reached over and eased back the side of the blanket. "Does he have any kind of birthmark?" The baby was wearing a blue one-piece suit so it was hard to see much of him.

Vickie nodded. "It's red. The shape of a strawberry."

Hell.

Because he had no choice, Austin hit the brakes and pulled off onto the shoulder. He reached for the baby, to see if the birthmark was in the right spot, but his hand felt rough and tight. Too rough to be touching a baby.

Thankfully, Rosalie did it for him.

The little boy had fallen asleep, but Rosalie gently opened the snaps and pushed the fabric away from his left leg.

It was there.

In the exact spot where his sister had said it would be.

"He's my nephew," Austin heard himself say, though he wasn't sure how he managed to speak. There was a huge lump in his throat now, and the muscles in his chest were too tight for him to breathe.

"I can drive," Rosalie suggested.

Obviously, she'd noticed this had hit him like a heavyweight's punch. So many emotions, including sheer relief, all coming at him at once. He'd done what he had promised his sister—he'd found Nathan.

Austin shook his head. "No, I can do this." He didn't want them out in the open any longer. "I can call my sister once we're in Sweetwater Springs."

Then, he could also start the process of having the baby tested so they'd have definitive proof.

Still, Austin felt the proof in his gut.

This was his missing nephew.

He got the truck moving again, trying not to hurry, but that's exactly what he wanted to do.

"Sweetwater Springs?" Vickie questioned. "We can't go there. I can't trust the sheriff."

Rosalie pulled back her shoulders. "You mean Cooper McKinnon?"

Vickie frantically nodded again. "He's the son

of the people involved in this. I looked him up on the internet, and I know he's their son."

The color drained from Rosalie's face. "What are you talking about?"

"It was their name on the agency paperwork," Vickie insisted. "Roy and Jewell McKinnon. They're the ones who arranged to adopt this baby."

Oh, no. Austin definitely didn't like the sound of that.

"That can't be right," Rosalie insisted, and she kept repeating it.

Austin wanted to reach over and try to reassure her that this could all be some kind of misunderstanding, that there was no way her parents or brother could be involved in this, but he saw the blur of motion just ahead.

A large SUV pulled directly out in front of them.

And it stopped right in the middle of the road.

Austin had to slam on his brakes. Not good since the roads were slick, and he went into a skid. He did a quick check of his rearview mirror to make sure Hernandez was still following them. He was. But the cop appeared to be fighting to keep control of his patrol car, too.

"Hold on," Austin warned them, praying that they didn't have a collision. The baby wasn't even in a car seat and could be hurt in just a fender bender.

Pumping the brakes and steering into the skid, Austin managed to stop the truck. Barely in time. But he didn't have time to do anything else.

Because two men jumped from the SUV.

They were armed, wearing ski masks, and both men aimed guns right at them.

"Get down!" But Austin didn't wait for Rosalie and Vickie to do that. He pushed them down on the seat and got ready to return fire.

"Oh, God," Rosalie whispered. "I think it's the guards from the second baby farm."

Yeah. But it didn't matter who they were. There was no way Austin would let them get their hands on Rosalie or his nephew.

Hernandez managed to stop just inches behind the truck. Austin opened his door, still using it for cover, got out and trained his own gun on the men. Hernandez did the same.

"All we want is the nanny," one of the masked guys snarled. His voice sounded firm enough, but he was volleying nervous glances between Austin and the detective. So was his partner. They probably hadn't expected to encounter two lawmen.

"Don't let them take me," Vickie begged.

Austin had no intention of letting that happen,

but what he didn't want was a gunfight with Rosalie and the baby caught in the middle.

"Put down your guns," Austin warned the men.

Again, the pair gave each other uneasy looks, and that upped Austin's own concern. He hoped like the devil that he could trust the lawman behind him. If not, Rosalie, Vickie and he were in a lot of trouble.

"If you don't give us the nanny," one of the men said, "we start shooting."

The nanny. But not the baby. "Why do they want only you?" Austin asked Vickie.

"I don't know. Maybe because I learned about the fake adoption agency."

Maybe. Or maybe this was all a ploy to make Vickie look innocent.

Either way, Austin prayed those men didn't pull their triggers, but just in case they did, he readied himself for the worst. One of the men backed up as if he might jump into the SUV and leave. Not the best solution, but it could be the only way to stop a gunfight.

But that didn't happen.

The idiot pulled the trigger, the shot blasting through the air and landing in the front bumper of the truck.

Austin cursed and did what he'd hoped he wouldn't have to do—he returned fire. So did

Detective Hernandez, and Austin heard him calling for backup. He also heard the baby's cries. The gunshot had woken him up.

Both masked men hurried behind their SUV. Both shooting into the truck. Austin wanted nothing more than to take them out, but he couldn't stay where he was. He had no choice but to jump back into his truck so he wouldn't be gunned down. Staying alive was the only way he could protect Rosalie and the others.

"I don't want them to hurt the baby," Vickie said. "I'll go with them."

Even though the adrenaline was spiking through him and he was concentrating on the attack, that set off alarms inside Austin's head. Maybe Vickie was just being protective of the baby, but he had to wonder if she wanted to go with them because she was part of their operation.

But if so, then why had she called Austin?

Again, it could have been to throw suspicion off herself. Maybe she knew that Yancy had brought up her name and that it made her a person of interest. Sonny could have even told her about Yancy's allegation.

"You'll stay put," Austin insisted, and he put the truck in gear and tried to maneuver around the SUV.

Hard to do with the SUV taking up most of the road.

It also didn't help that the cruiser was right behind him. That didn't give Austin much room to move. He threw the truck into Reverse, backing up as much as he could so he could drive onto the shoulder.

Rosalie levered herself up, placing her body in front of the baby. Protecting his nephew. He hated that she was forced to do that, but there wasn't an alternative. They had to protect the little boy. Those bullets could come through the engine and into the cab of the truck. And as an adult, she stood a better chance of surviving an injury like that.

The shoulder of the road was nothing more than gravel and ice, and the truck tires on the passenger's side wobbled, threatening to send them straight into the ditch. That couldn't happen because then they'd be sitting ducks.

The gunmen were still behind cover of their SUV. Still shooting. But they were aiming for the tires now. At least they weren't shooting at them, but it was still a dangerous situation. Plus, the gunmen were moving, adjusting their positions so that they could get a better shot at stopping them.

Austin cursed. He hadn't come this far to rescue his nephew only to have the gunmen snatch him away again. And despite their insistence that they only wanted Vickie, Austin figured the plan was to get both her and the baby back while they eliminated Rosalie, him and the cop.

Behind him, Hernandez jumped into his cruiser, backing up just enough to give Austin some room to maneuver. Still, the tires shimmied over the slick surface, and he couldn't get enough traction.

The bullets kept coming, and he felt one slam into the front tire on the driver's side. That's when Austin knew he couldn't wait any longer.

"Hold on," he warned Rosalie and Vickie, and he hit the button to disable the air bags. He couldn't risk having them deploy and hurting the baby. A split second later, he floored the accelerator.

The front end of the truck bashed into the SUV and sent it crashing into the gunmen. It knocked them both to the ground. But only temporarily. They came up ready to fire.

Austin pressed hard on the gas again. The truck fishtailed, and the partially deflated front tire didn't help matters. He had to wrestle with the steering wheel to keep the vehicle on the road.

Behind him, he saw the detective doing the same. Trying to get the heck out of there. Maybe it wouldn't be long before backup arrived, and the gunmen could be arrested.

But not by Austin.

He couldn't risk the lives of the people inside his truck. However, this was definitely a score he intended to settle later.

Austin cleared the SUV, pushed hard on the accelerator and drove away, the bullets still coming at them.

Chapter Nine

"You should go home and let me handle this," Rosalie's brother Seth insisted—again.

He was using that overly protective brother tone that Rosalie both loved and hated.

At the moment, she felt more of the latter.

Rosalie totally understood his concern. After all, it had been only a few hours since Austin and she had been caught in that gunfight, but attacks like that wouldn't stop unless she found answers about who those men were behind the masks.

"I want to hear what Mom has to say," Rosalie insisted right back—again.

If her mother knew anything about the baby farms or Austin's nephew, then Rosalie wanted to hear it from Jewell's own lips.

And find out why her mother hadn't volunteered it to her sooner.

That's why Rosalie had insisted on coming to the jail to have this chat with her mother.

Of course, Vickie could be and likely was lying about her parents' involvement. Or worse. Vickie could be the culprit behind the baby farms, and the attack could have been orchestrated to make her seem innocent. That's why the FBI was questioning her.

Not Austin, though.

His boss had refused to let him have any part of that when they'd shown up at the FBI building shortly after the latest attack. Probably a good thing, too, since he had a much happier task of reuniting his sister with her son. The reunion wouldn't be an official one until the DNA test results were back, but Rosalie knew with all her heart that the child was indeed back where he belonged.

It was bittersweet for her.

On the one hand it gave her hope that she'd be reunited with her own baby, but the waiting was crushing her like deadweight.

Seth checked the latest text that popped onto his phone screen, glanced around, no doubt wondering what was taking so long. Rosalie and he hadn't had an appointment for this jail visit, and according to the warden, their mother was tied up with some kind of statement with her lawyer. Rosalie didn't care how long the wait would be. She wasn't budging.

"Anything on the investigation?" she asked

when Seth's attention went back to the text. "Have they found those gunmen who got away?"

Seth shook his head to both questions, and even though he didn't make a sound, she could feel his frustration. Mixed with her own, the visiting room at the county jail was heavy with it and all the other emotions coursing through her.

"Vickie refused protective custody," Seth added a moment later.

"Why?" After the attack, Rosalie couldn't imagine the woman doing that. Unless Vickie truly had nothing to fear from the gunmen, that is. But if Vickie had been the person in control of the baby farms, she should have at least accepted protective custody so she wouldn't appear guilty.

"Vickie says she doesn't trust cops," Seth explained. "But I also get the feeling that she plans to do some investigating of her own. Maybe you can tell her what a really dumb idea that'd be."

She gave him an obligatory smirk.

Seth gave her one in return, and he was better at smirking than she was. "After you talk to Mom, you'll go back to the ranch."

Rosalie didn't look at him because he would see in her eyes that she had no intention of doing that. Or of giving up on the search for her baby. She just kept her attention on the glass where she hoped her mother would soon appear.

"Are you ever going to tell me how you got involved in this mess?" Seth asked.

"I would, but you won't like it, and right now, we both have enough to deal with."

That earned her a glare that she could see in the reflection of the glass. It earned her some profanity, too. "Did you do anything illegal?"

Rosalie lifted her shoulder. "I used your home computer to find the criminal informant who helped me get the job at the baby farm."

"*My* computer," he flatly repeated. "The one I didn't password protect because I didn't think my sister would go snooping on it?"

"Yes, that computer," Rosalie mumbled. The one he kept in the ranch guesthouse that they shared.

Oh, that made his glare even worse. "And let me guess—the reason you asked me to give you shooting lessons about two months ago was because of this?"

Since it was true, Rosalie settled for another shoulder lift. "I needed two things to start my plan to find Sadie. A way into the baby farm operation and a way to defend myself if something went wrong."

And things had indeed gone wrong.

Seth would have no doubt given her another scowling reminder about that, followed by another lecture, if his phone hadn't buzzed. When he glanced at the name on the screen, it instantly brought him to his feet.

"I have to take this, and it might be a long conversation," he said, shielding the phone screen from her before he stepped outside the room.

She hadn't seen the caller's name, but maybe because Seth was about to learn yet something else that she wouldn't want to hear. This way, he could try to shelter her, something he'd been doing since this nightmare had started eleven months ago. But sheltering wasn't going to help. Only finding Sadie and the truth would do that.

Rosalie stared at the glass, trying to tamp down the wild thoughts that kept zinging through her head. And she kept going back to one huge question. If her parents had had some part in this, why hadn't they told her?

Certainly not because they were behind the baby farms.

No, she was sure of that.

Until recently, Rosalie and her father, Roy, had been estranged for over twenty years—since her mother had left the ranch under a cloud of suspicion about an affair and rumors of murdering her lover. A murder accusation that had put Jewell behind bars while she waited for a murder trial. But her mother was innocent of the crime. Innocent of the baby farms, too.

Still, Rosalie couldn't get Vickie's accusation to quit eating away at her.

The visiting room door eased open, and Rosalie braced herself for Seth's return with more bad news. But it wasn't her brother who stepped in.

It was Austin.

Her heart went straight to her throat. "Did something go wrong?" And just like that, so many bad possibilities came to mind. "Did someone kidnap your nephew again? Did they find the men who attacked us?"

"No to all of it." He shook his head, seemed a little surprised by her questions. "My nephew's fine and with my sister at our family's ranch." Austin showed her the photo on his phone. A woman smiling through her happy tears as she clutched her baby in her arms.

The relief came as quickly as the dread and fear, and before she even realized she was going to do it, Rosalie threw her arms around him. That obviously surprised him, too, judging from the way his muscles tensed.

Then quickly relaxed.

That caused Rosalie to tense, as well, because they shouldn't feel this comfortable in each other's arms. Even if she did. And worse, not just comfortable.

But safe.

Austin kept his hand on her waist even after she came to her senses and eased away from him.

"Sorry," she said. "But when I saw you, I thought the worst."

Austin flexed his eyebrows, and the corner of his mouth lifted. "That's not usually the reaction I'm aiming for." But he quickly shook his head. "I can understand it in your case, though."

That half smile sent another trickle of heat through her, but Rosalie decided to blame it on the fact that he hadn't come to deliver bad news. It'd been a while since she'd heard anything good, and a baby reunited with his mother definitely qualified as good.

"What about Detective Hernandez?" she pressed. "Is he all right?"

"Fine. A little shaken up, of course. SAPD is out looking for the men who shot at us. The plates on their SUV were fake, though, so that's a dead end."

Rosalie had already expected that. The men had come there to attack them. Maybe to kidnap Vickie and the baby, too. Unless they were idiots, they wouldn't have used a vehicle that could be traced back to them. That was also the reason they'd worn masks—to conceal their identities.

"But why did you come?" she asked.

No more half smile, but he did give another flex of his eyebrows. "To help you find your daughter."

The old wounds and bad blood instantly made her suspicious. "I've already told you that you don't owe me anything."

Now his gaze came to hers.

Oh, no.

She saw it then. That same blasted trickle of heat that she felt in her own body. Rosalie muttered some profanity.

"It's not just *that*," Austin corrected. Thankfully, he didn't clarify what he meant. "Well, not totally that, anyway. I'm already familiar with the investigation. And I have some time on my hands since I'm on a thirty-day suspension." He took her by the shoulders when she looked away. "I *need* to help you."

No doubt to relieve the guilt over Eli's death. But that wasn't the only source of guilt in the room. This unwanted attraction made her feel as if she were cheating on Eli even though he'd been dead well over a year and a half. Being around Austin wasn't likely to ease the heat or the guilt, either.

And that's why it was best if they parted ways.

She heard the footsteps. Again, not Seth. These came from the other side of the building, and a moment later, Rosalie spotted the guard ushering her mother into the visiting area.

"Rosalie, I'm sorry I kept you waiting," Jewell said, her voice as thin and weak as she appeared. The orange prison jumpsuit swallowed her and washed out her color even more than it already was. "My lawyer had some good news. A witness has come forward who might be able to clear my name. I don't know all the details yet, but we should know more soon."

It was news Rosalie hadn't expected, but it was indeed welcome. She was about to press for the identity of the witness, but Jewell spoke before she could.

"Something's wrong," she said, looking first at Rosalie and then at Austin.

"Maybe," Rosalie settled for saying. She tipped her head to Austin. "Do you remember Agent Duran?"

"Of course. Eli's former partner. How are you, Austin?" If there was any hint that her mother blamed Austin for Eli's death, it certainly wasn't in her voice. She was warm and welcoming, as if greeting him at her home rather than the county jail.

"I'm fine. Thank you."

"Good." Jewell gave them both another looking over. "I suspect I owe you a thanks for taking care of my daughter. I don't know the details, but judging from your expressions and the fact that the guard said Seth is here, too, you've had a *difficult* morning." She paused. "And you think I can help in some way?"

"I was, uh, doing some investigating," Rosalie started. "I ran into Austin, and we met a woman. Vickie Cravens."

The name hung in the air for several moments, and Jewell shook her head. "You think I know her?"

"She said you did." Rosalie had to clear her throat to continue. "She's a nanny and claimed Roy and you were going to adopt a baby that she was keeping."

"Oh." Jewell pulled in a quick breath.

Sweet heaven. Her mother certainly wasn't denying it.

"The baby was my nephew," Austin added. "Were you aware of that?"

"No, absolutely not." Jewell pressed her hand to her throat as if to steady herself. "But Roy and I have been working together to find Sadie since she was first kidnapped."

"What do you mean?" This was the first Rosalie was hearing about that. "Working together?"

Jewell nodded. "You were heartbroken, crushed, and I knew I had to do something to get Sadie back. Roy has contacts in law enforcement, so I called him. After that, we met a few times to discuss what to do."

"You okay?" Austin whispered to her, and it took Rosalie a moment to realize she had gone board-stiff. Austin slipped his hand over hers, and this time Rosalie didn't move away from him.

"There's a lot of bad blood between my parents," she mumbled. So much, in fact, that she figured Roy was the last man on earth who'd help her mother.

"Roy and I split up twenty-three years ago," Jewell explained. "It's a long story."

Not really. Rosalie could summarize it in just one sentence. "Roy believed my mother had an affair, and amid rumors that she'd murdered her lover, Roy kicked her, me and my sister off the family ranch."

Even now, that was still an open wound for her, and it was the reason she still hadn't been able to call Roy her father. Painful baggage indeed, though she was trying to get past it. Only because she had more immediate matters to handle—finding her baby and stopping her mother from being wrongfully convicted of murder.

"After the rumors of the murder, Roy and I decided to divorce," Jewell corrected. "And I took my twin daughters with me. Rosalie and her sister were young, barely six years old. But our boys were older and could speak for themselves. They wanted to stay with their father, so Roy raised them."

Unlike Rosalie, there was no bitterness in Jewell's tone or body language, but Rosalie figured it had to be there somewhere under all that calm composure. Despite the rose-colored spin her mother had just put on things, Rosalie believed that Roy had demanded that she leave.

"Five months or so after Sadie was taken," Jewell continued, "Roy and I were worried when the cops and FBI weren't finding anything. So, we put out the word through some shady sources that we were looking to buy a baby. One that we hoped to use to help heal Rosalie's heart."

"That wouldn't have happened," Rosalie jumped to say.

"I know," her mother assured her. "But we thought saying that might convince the person behind the black market adoptions. And it did, I guess. Weeks later, someone finally called Roy using a voice scrambler, and whoever it was used a prepaid cell that couldn't be traced. The person said someone would contact Roy when they had a baby for us."

Rosalie hadn't suspected any of this. Of course, she'd been so involved with her own search and her own pain that she wasn't looking for clues that her mother had been doing the same thing.

With Roy's help, no less.

Rosalie remembered something else and shook her head. "But Vickie knew your names. She said you were to adopt Austin's nephew. Why did you ask for a boy if you were looking for Sadie?"

"We didn't ask for a specific baby. If we had, we would have asked for a baby Sadie's own age, but we thought that would make them believe we were only searching for our granddaughter. Instead, we said we wanted to adopt a child. Any child." Her mother stopped again, gathered her breath. "Roy paid them twenty-five thousand through a wire transfer to an offshore account with the agreement that they'd get another twenty-five grand once we had the baby."

Fifty thousand. That was the going rate for one of these babies? It sickened Rosalie to think of these monsters selling babies for cash. There was no price tag she could put on her precious daughter.

"Finally, Roy and I got a call that a baby boy was ready for adoption, and that we could have him within a week," her mother went on. "We were told to wait and that we'd get instructions about the pickup and how to make the final payment. After I was arrested, the person didn't contact us again."

Her mother's arrest had happened nearly four

months ago. Right about the time that Austin's nephew had been kidnapped.

Maybe the arrest had scared off the baby broker?

That had to be it because these baby sellers wouldn't have cared if the arrest made Jewell an unsuitable mother. However, they might have thought Roy would be under some kind of police surveillance.

Austin added some profanity under his breath and gave Jewell a hard stare. "I can't believe Seth would have let you do something like that. It was dangerous. The person behind this could have killed both of you."

"Seth didn't know. *Doesn't* know," Jewell corrected, her cheeks flushing a little. "I'd like to keep it that way, especially since the deal didn't go through. And if it had, we would have gladly brought in Seth, Cooper and anyone else to catch these monsters. We would have done anything to rescue not only that child but any others we might have found."

Rosalie and Austin exchanged another glance, and she saw the questions in his eyes. If Yancy was indeed behind the baby farms, then he could have targeted Austin's nephew to give to Roy and Jewell. A way to dig the knife in even deeper to punish Austin for the investigation that had nearly landed Yancy in jail.

But if so, it was risky, too, since Yancy must have suspected that her parents would have just turned the baby over to the authorities. Of course, Yancy would have still gotten the fifty grand. He was a rich man, but he probably wouldn't have turned down the cash, and besides he could have had plans just to kidnap the baby boy again. Or scam another set of prospective parents into paying for a baby they'd never get.

"Roy and I didn't tell anyone what we'd done," Jewell went on, "because we thought someone might be monitoring our phone calls. Or at least keeping an eye on us. They likely wanted to make sure what we were doing wasn't some kind of a setup. If we'd told you or Seth, we were afraid it would have blown the deal."

Instead, her mother's arrest had blown it.

The door opened, and Seth walked back in. With one sweeping glance, he took in the whole room, no doubt noticing Jewell's troubled expression.

And the way Austin was holding Rosalie's hand.

"Bad news?" Austin asked, getting to his feet so he could face Seth.

Seth shook his head. "We found something. We might finally have some proof of the person who set up the baby farm."

Chapter Ten

Sonny.

Austin hated that the man's name kept popping up in all the wrong places. Here Sonny had been out of jail only a few hours on the gun charges, but this was a new reason to bring him right back in. Austin had read through the financial report and saw the same red flags that Seth had.

Something wasn't right on several levels.

For one thing Sonny had two offshore accounts—not exactly standard practice for a run-of-the-mill P.I. Then, there were the cash transfers and withdrawals from his Texas bank. Not enough to trigger an investigation. Just enough to keep him under the radar of the authorities.

Or at least it would have been enough if he hadn't become a person of interest in the baby farms investigation.

"It all seems, well, almost too obvious," Rosalie said, studying the financial report from over Austin's shoulder. "I mean, if Sonny's behind the baby farms, why would he leave this kind of evidence out there for someone to find?"

Austin made a sound of agreement. "But then, Sonny's done plenty of *too obvious*. Like being at the second site of the baby farm and pulling a gun on Yancy at the hospital. All of that makes him look guilty."

And in doing so, it also made him look innocent and as if he'd been set up. Either by Yancy or someone else.

Rosalie must have come to the same conclusion because she huffed and sank back in the chair next to him. Her brother Cooper, the sheriff of Sweetwater Springs, had been generous enough to let them use his private office to go through the financials while they waited for Sonny to arrive for questioning.

Yet something else that was generous.

If Cooper hadn't allowed Austin and Seth to question Sonny at the sheriff's office, then it would have had to be moved to the FBI building in San Antonio. Where Austin wouldn't have been allowed even to witness the interview much less take part in it.

"I owe your brother Cooper," Austin mumbled.

Rosalie made another sound, not one of agreement this time. "I was surprised that he allowed it. Cooper isn't exactly on good terms with Seth, my sister and me."

Austin didn't have to ask why. They'd been raised by their mother. Cooper and his brothers, by their father. After twenty-something years of estrangement, that was a huge rift to mend.

"So, why then did Cooper let us come here?" Austin asked.

She shrugged, glanced away when Austin tried to make eye contact with her. "I think he feels sorry for me. Like you do," she added.

Austin did feel sorry for her, but sadly, it wasn't the only thing he was feeling for her. Ditto for the guilt. Every time he looked at her—like now—he got that jolt of a reminder that Rosalie was a darn attractive woman.

The jolt was put on hold fast when the door flew open and Seth poked in his head. "Sonny's on his way. Should be here in the next ten minutes or so, and he's bringing his attorney."

"He should," Austin agreed. "If Sonny doesn't have a solid explanation for what's in that financial report, then he could end up in jail again."

Even though this was just an interview for the man, the stakes were sky-high. Not only for Sonny but for all of them. Because Sonny might surprise them all and confess to everything.

Seth shrugged. "I don't care who I have to

arrest as long as Rosalie stays safe. After the interview, you'll take her back to the ranch."

"Of course," Austin said as at the same time Rosalie argued, "I can get myself back to the ranch."

"Those guards from the baby farm are still out there," Austin quickly reminded her.

She didn't continue to argue, but Austin could still see the uneasiness that she felt about being around him. Seth mumbled a thanks and left, shutting the door behind him.

Austin figured this was a subject that he should just let die, but he couldn't seem to make himself shut up. "When you look at me, do you think of Eli?"

Rosalie didn't jump to answer. In fact, she turned away from him, her gaze going to the window.

"I'm sorry," he added. "If I could change that, I would. You don't know how many times I've wished that I'd been the one to die that night."

Still no verbal response, but she swallowed hard. "I used to want that. But in a perfect world, you both would have lived, and Yancy or who-ever else was responsible for that attack would have been arrested."

Austin had to mentally replay that, and he took her by the arm and eased her around to face him. "You mean that?"

She nodded, swallowed hard again. "And when I look at you, I don't think of Eli. That's the problem."

He replayed that, too, and even if he hadn't been looking her straight in the eyes, he still would have realized what she meant.

Rosalie was talking about this attraction between them. He'd felt it, of course. And like her had fought it like crazy. Because it didn't make sense. Even if he could dismiss the bad blood that'd been between them, they were still in the middle of a dangerous investigation. Hardly the time to start lusting after someone.

"For what it's worth," Austin said, "it's a problem for me, too."

Since that only revved up the concern in her eyes, Austin wanted to put his arms around her. To tell her that everything would be okay. But with the fire and energy zinging between them, that wasn't a good idea.

Did that stop him?

No.

When it came to Rosalie, he just didn't seem to have a lick of sense. He tugged her closer, fully expecting her to hold her ground and keep her distance.

She didn't.

Rosalie landed in his arms as if it were the most natural thing in the world. It felt as if she belonged there, too, and it didn't help cool down the heat.

"This is a mistake," he heard himself say.

It was. That didn't stop him. Austin lowered his head and put his mouth on hers.

He'd braced himself for the guilt and all the other feelings he'd expected. However, those didn't come. He was too wrapped up in the avalanche of sensations. The softness of her lips. Her taste.

That silky little moan that purred in her throat.

All those things slammed through him, and just like that, he was starved for her and had to have more. Austin slid his hand around the back of her neck, deepening the kiss and pulling her closer and closer to him.

Mercy, she tasted good.

Felt even better.

Rosalie did her own share of deepening. She lifted her hands, first one and then the other, sliding them around his neck and completing the body-to-body contact between them.

Not good in a bad way.

He could feel her breasts. Could feel her heart thudding against his chest. And, of course, he could feel the need brewing. It wasn't something he'd ever expected from her.

Or from himself.

But here it was. Strong, hot and getting hotter with each passing second.

Austin forced himself to back away. Not easy. The majority of his body yelled at him to go right back for more, but he wanted to give her a chance to catch her breath and rethink this mistake they were making.

He saw the surprise in her mist-gray eyes, but the heat was there in abundance, as well.

"You can slap me if it'll help," he offered. Austin hoped his god-awful attempt at levity would ease the sudden tension between them.

It didn't.

"I don't think anything will help." She groaned and stepped away from him. "This shouldn't be happening."

All Austin could do was nod in agreement. "If I could stop it, I would, but the truth is, I've always been attracted to you."

He expected her to laugh or give him the slap that she'd said wouldn't help, but Rosalie just stared at him. Then, she nodded.

"You knew that?" he asked.

Another tentative nod. "But I also knew you wouldn't act on it because of Eli, because he was your partner and friend."

Well, heck.

All this time he'd thought he had done a decent job of covering up his feelings for her.

Apparently, he sucked as much at that as he did at resisting her now.

"I can't promise you that I won't kiss you again," Austin confessed.

Rosalie stared at him as if she might try to convince him otherwise, but the door flew open again, and Seth looked in at them. They stepped away from each other as if they'd been caught doing something wrong. Not far from the truth.

And Seth noticed all right.

Maybe because Rosalie's breathing still hadn't leveled, her mouth was slightly swollen from the kissing and their faces were no doubt flushed.

Seth didn't have to tell them that Sonny was there because Austin immediately heard the man's voice. And not just Sonny's, either, but another voice that he hadn't expected to hear.

"Yancy came with him?" Austin automatically stepped in front of Rosalie.

"Yeah," Seth verified. "Sonny said he's got proof that it's really Yancy behind the baby farms, and he wanted him at the sheriff's office so all of us could hear it."

Austin groaned. If there was indeed proof, then he would welcome it, but he didn't want to go another round with these two bozos. Not with Rosalie so close, anyway.

"I can handle this if you'd like," Seth offered.

This time Rosalie and Austin answered in

unison, and they were clearly on the same page. "No," they said.

Even though Austin would have preferred Rosalie to stay out of this, he wouldn't try to force her to do that. Not that he could have, anyway. She would do anything to find her daughter. Including facing down the man who might have been responsible for Eli's death.

Austin stepped out ahead of Seth and aimed glares at both Yancy and Sonny while the sheriff and his deputy were frisking the men for weapons. "If either of you draws a gun," Austin warned both Sonny and Yancy, "I'll be the one to shoot first, and I'll put you in the cemetery, not the hospital. You both got that?"

Sonny gave a crisp nod, but Yancy only chuckled. "Same ol' Agent Duran. Always was too high-strung for me. Same with this one." He hitched his thumb to Sonny. "And now he's here to accuse me once again of something I didn't do. Brought his ambulance-chasing lawyer with him, too."

"I'm Patrick Donald," the lawyer said. He was young, probably barely out of law school, and looked more like a linebacker than a lawyer, which meant he likely doubled as Sonny's muscle or bodyguard.

Since this could easily launch into a full-scale argument, Austin motioned for the men to follow Seth, Rosalie and him to the interview room. He'd start with them together at first. An unofficial chat since he couldn't conduct an official one. Then, Yancy and Sonny could be separated so that Seth could take actual statements.

Or if they got very lucky, confessions.

Austin would like nothing more than to have these two locked up so the attacks against Rosalie would stop and she could be reunited with Sadie.

Sonny moved slowly, clutching his arm. No doubt because of the gunshot wound. Austin wasn't about to have any sympathy for the man though because Sonny could have gotten that injury while operating the baby farm. Of course, Austin might change his mind about that sympathy if Sonny came through on giving them info they could actually use.

"Before you give us this proof about Yancy's guilt," Austin started, looking at Sonny, "explain your own *guilt*."

He stepped into the room with the men but didn't go far, mainly so he could keep Rosalie in the doorway in case something went wrong. Yes, they'd been searched for weapons, but that didn't mean they couldn't have somehow sneaked one in.

"You mean the financials you have on my client," the lawyer volunteered. He fumbled with the papers that he pulled from a folder he was holding. "The offshore holdings are bogus. My client had nothing to do with those."

"You can prove that?" Seth asked, maneuvering around his sister to join Austin shoulder to shoulder.

Seth had probably made that adjustment in his position for the same reason that Austin had—to try to shield Rosalie. But it didn't work. She came right in next to her brother and Austin.

"I can prove it with time," the lawyer insisted. "But my client shouldn't have to go to such measures. He's innocent, and someone is obviously setting him up." Donald's gaze shifted to Yancy, where his accusing glare landed.

"There you go again," Yancy griped. "Trying to put the blame on me, like always."

Austin cut Yancy off with a quick slicing motion of his hand and kept his attention pinned to Sonny. One battle at a time, and he was nowhere near done with Sonny.

"What about the deposits and withdrawals in your U.S. account? Did someone fake those, too?" Austin asked.

"No," Donald said, speaking for his client. "Those were legitimate expenditures and deposits for my client's P.I. business, and you can contact his accountant if you have specific questions."

"Oh, we'll contact him all right," Austin assured him, and he hoped it sounded like the threat that it was. If there was any dirt to find on Sonny, he intended to find it.

"Did you take my daughter?" Rosalie asked, obviously aiming the question at Sonny.

"No," Sonny immediately answered. His lawyer caught on to his arms, no doubt to stop him from saying anything else, but Sonny just shook off the man's grip. "But I'm pretty sure Yancy did."

Sonny reached inside his coat, and the gesture prompted both Seth and Austin to draw their guns. Yancy laughed again, but Sonny lifted his hands.

"I was just taking out the proof you'll need to put this piece of slime behind bars," Sonny insisted.

Austin gave him the go-ahead nod, but neither he nor Seth put away their firearms until he saw that it was indeed just an envelope that Sonny took from his inside coat pocket. Sonny opened it, took out three photos and spread them on the metal table in front of him.

All three pictures were grainy, as if taken from a long-range camera lens, but Austin had no trouble recognizing the place.

It was the baby farm where Rosalie and he had been.

"No!" Yancy practically shouted, and he reached as if to snatch up the photos, but Seth blocked him from doing that.

Both Austin and Rosalie moved closer for a better look at what had prompted Yancy's reaction. It didn't take Austin long to figure it out.

Yancy was in all three of the photos.

"It was a setup," Yancy snarled. "I thought I was meeting a business associate there who was interested in buying the property from me. Now I see that was a ruse to get so-called proof of my involvement in this mess."

Rosalie and Austin exchanged glances. "You own the baby farm?" she asked Yancy.

Yancy opened his mouth, closed it, and he stuffed his hands in his pockets. "One of my corporations owns the land and rents it out," he finally said, as if choosing his words carefully. "I own dozens of properties. So many I don't even know where they all are."

"You own dummy corporations," Austin argued. "And there's no honest reason for that. Plenty of dishonest ones, though."

Yancy's smug look returned. "I don't like mixing apples and oranges, especially since my last divorce. Lost a boatload of money to that witch, so the corporations help me keep things, well, organized."

And it kept assets hidden so that he couldn't be readily identified for criminal activities.

"Who rented the baby farm?" Rosalie demanded. But she didn't just demand it. She stepped around Austin, went straight for Yancy and got right in his face.

Yancy met her stare. "I don't know."

"He's lying." Sonny got to his feet and jabbed his index finger at the pictures. "He was there. He knows what's going on because he's the one behind it."

"I'm not behind it. That's the truth," Yancy added when Seth, Austin and she groaned. A muscle flickered in his jaw. "I'm not the only one who structures their business with corporations."

"What the heck does that mean?" Austin snapped.

"It means my people didn't do a thorough job of checking out the person who rented that ranch property for the baby farm. Or checking out the person who set me up for those photos. The names are all fake, part of a dummy corporation."

"Convenient," Austin mumbled, and he cursed.

Rosalie looked as if she wanted to curse, too. Or cry. This had to feel like another blow to her heart. Yet another stone wall in the investigation. Still, they might be able to chip at this wall and figure out what was behind it.

"You'll give us everything you know about your own corporations," Austin told Yancy. "Including the one you claim set you up."

Austin expected Yancy to argue since the FBI could use that info to uncover criminal activity, but after several snail-crawling moments, the man finally nodded. "I'll have my lawyer deliver anything that might apply here to the sheriff's office."

Now it was Sonny who cursed. "Anything he gives you will be fake. All lies."

"You mean like those photos?" Yancy fired back. "Seems like you're doing way too much finger-pointing, Sonny-boy. If you ask me, you're acting like a guilty man with all these wild accusations."

That set off another round of arguing, and Austin moved Rosalie out of the middle. Seth took over, issuing both men threats if they didn't settle down. He also motioned for Austin to get Rosalie out of there. Austin was about to do just that when his phone buzzed.

"It's Vickie," Austin whispered to Rosalie after glancing down at the screen. Since there was no way he wanted Yancy or Sonny to hear the conversation, he took Rosalie into the hall and shut the door.

"Are you okay?" Austin greeted Vickie when he answered. He hoped those baby farm guards hadn't come after her, though it was a possibility since Vickie had refused protective custody.

"I'm scared." That fear came through loud and clear in her voice. "I remembered something about your nephew and the man who brought him to me."

"What?" Austin asked. Rosalie obviously heard what the woman said because she pulled in her breath, waiting.

"Something important," Vickie said. "But I can't get into it over the phone. We need to meet because I have something to show you."

Chapter Eleven

While she paced, Rosalie listened for Austin's phone, willing it to ring.

Something that she'd been doing for the past hour.

It shouldn't be hard to hear the ringing sound because the guest cottage at the ranch wasn't large, since it was just two small bedrooms, a bath, a living room and kitchen. Not nearly enough space to put much distance between Austin and her.

Unfortunately, though, it'd been just enough for her not to hear all of his phone conversations. And he'd had plenty of those. For each one, Austin had spoken in hushed tones, never putting the calls on speaker, probably in the hopes of not disturbing her.

It hadn't worked.

Nothing would at this point except finding her baby and putting an end to the danger.

Since Austin was sleeping on the sofa in the

living room, Rosalie wasn't pacing in there but rather in the kitchen, and she figured the pacing wouldn't end until the phone rang. It was only six in the morning, and since Vickie hadn't given them a specific time when she would call to arrange a meeting, it didn't necessarily mean there was reason for alarm yet.

Still, Rosalie was just that—alarmed.

She wanted the woman to call so they could meet her and see whatever it was she wanted to show them. And she wanted Vickie to do that before anything else went wrong. Whoever was behind the baby farm would likely attack Vickie and anyone else who tried to shed light on the illegal adoptions. Unless Vickie was setting up this meeting so that Austin and she could be silenced. Since that was a possibility, it'd mean they would have to take plenty more precautions.

Including emotional precautions on her part.

Especially since the reason for her emotional precautions was only a few feet away. Rosalie kept her footsteps as light as she could and paced closer to the living room so she could get another glimpse of the cowboy on the couch.

And even while sleeping, Austin was definitely still a cowboy.

He had his black Stetson slung over his face, and he was still wearing his jeans and boots.

The sofa was too short for him, so his feet were propped up on the armrest. He looked ready to jump right into action.

Well, except for that unbuttoned shirt.

Rosalie didn't want to notice his chest, but she did, anyway. That chest looked as if he knew his way around a gym, but she suspected it'd come from working hard on his family's ranch. It was definitely a body that got her attention.

She touched her fingertips to her mouth, remembering the kiss that shouldn't have happened. She hadn't even tried to resist him but instead had stayed there in Austin's arms while he stirred the heat inside her.

The heat was still stirring.

And that unbuttoned shirt sure didn't help.

She silently groaned, forced herself to look away. Soon, very soon, after they'd dealt with Vickie's possible news, Rosalie would have to figure out a way to make Austin understand that this wasn't his fight. She appreciated his help, but being close to him like this just wasn't a good idea.

Because she was falling for him.

That caused her to mumble some profanity, and she turned to go back into the kitchen.

"You don't have to leave. I'm awake," Austin said, without taking the Stetson from his face.

Even though he couldn't actually see her, he

might have figured out that she'd been gawking at him. That wouldn't help with the attraction, either, so Rosalie came up with a quick excuse. "I was just making sure that Vickie hadn't called."

"She hasn't." Austin added a groggy-sounding sigh and sat up. With his shirt still open. He tossed his Stetson on the coffee table and scrubbed his hand over his face.

"You should have taken Seth's bed," Rosalie commented. "He didn't make it in last night."

Of course, Austin already knew that. He'd taken a shower about five hours earlier before crashing on the couch, and he would have no doubt heard if Seth had come in since her brother would have had to walk right past him. Rosalie wasn't sure what'd kept Seth, but he was likely working on this investigation and had crashed at his office. Something he did more often than not.

"Should you try to call Vickie?" she asked.

"I did, about two hours ago. The call went straight to voice mail."

Oh, mercy. She prayed that meant nothing had gone wrong with Vickie, but with everything else going on, that was a strong possibility.

"You do know that you can't go to any meeting that Vickie sets up?" Austin asked. Except it wasn't exactly a question. More like a statement of fact.

"I need to go," she insisted. "I need to find out what she wants to show us."

Austin was shaking his head before she even finished. "I can't put you in that kind of danger again. Seth will go with me, and I'll wear a wire so you can hear what's going on. But you'll stay here at the ranch. Your brother Colt told me that the ranch hands are all armed, and that he'll make sure to be here when Seth and I are gone."

This was the first she was hearing of any of this. "Did you talk to Colt about this when we were at the sheriff's office yesterday?"

"No. About two hours ago. I called him. He's already set up some extra security and has ranch hands on patrol so that no one tries to use the fence to get onto the ranch."

So, he'd gotten even less sleep than she'd originally thought. And during his sleepless time, he'd managed to come up with a plan with her brother to exclude her from talking with Vickie.

Rosalie didn't like that, and she was ready to voice that displeasure when he stood, stretching and giving her an even better peek at the chest that she shouldn't be peeking at. She forced herself to look away. But not before Austin got a glimpse of her face.

"This is about that kiss, isn't it?" Austin

mumbled, but he didn't wait for her to confirm it. He strolled toward her, finally doing something about that unbuttoned shirt. "I should apologize."

Rosalie found herself dumbfounded again. It probably wasn't a good idea for them to be discussing the attraction, but when Austin reached her, he slid his hand around the back of her neck and pulled her to him for a brief but scalding-hot kiss.

"I should apologize for that, too." He made a sound as if he liked what he'd tasted, and his gaze landed on the coffeepot. "Thank God, caffeine."

He helped himself to a full mug while Rosalie stood there with what she was sure was a gob-smacked look on her face. He gulped some of the coffee down with his attention still on her.

"You hate me," he concluded.

"I hate myself," she countered. But then had to shake her head. "I'm just confused."

"About your feelings or me?"

She had to think about that a moment. "Both. You know we shouldn't be feeling these things, right?"

"Yeah, but I also know that wanting the attraction to stop doesn't work." He paused, had more coffee. "After we find Sadie and you get on with your life, maybe then you'll be able to forgive me."

"I have forgiven you. That's the problem. I've forgiven you, but I can't forgive myself for feeling this…guilt."

He nodded. "Part of me died that night, too, with Eli. But I'm not sure that's what he would have wanted."

It wasn't. Rosalie knew that in her heart, but she just couldn't let go. And that's why she stepped back when Austin reached for her again.

She got just a glimpse of the troubled look on his face before his phone rang. He hurried, grabbing it so fast that he nearly knocked it off the table.

"It's Vickie," he let her know as he answered it, and this time he put the call on speaker.

"Sorry that I didn't answer my phone, but I've been on the move since we talked," the woman immediately said. "Someone was following me when I tried to go back to the motel where I was staying."

Rosalie could hear the fear in her voice. Or rather Vickie *sounded* afraid. After everything they'd been through, Rosalie wasn't about to take that at face value. Vickie could be playing some kind of sick game with them.

"When and where are we meeting?" Austin demanded.

"I'm at the McKinnon ranch. Well, near it, anyway. I'm on the road just outside a closed cattle gate. If you open it, I can drive in and we can talk now."

Austin cursed. "You shouldn't have come here. That's too risky for you and Rosalie. Meet me at the sheriff's office in town."

"No. I told you I don't trust the cops. I'm not going there."

"You can trust the sheriff," Rosalie insisted. "He's my brother."

Now it was Vickie who cursed. "I don't care who he is. If you want the information I have, then open the cattle gate right now. If not, I disappear, and you'll never see what I have or me again."

Sweet heaven. Rosalie could practically feel the debate going on inside Austin because she, too, was having the same reaction.

She wanted to trust Vickie, but it was a huge risk to allow her onto the ranch. After all, she could still be working for the person behind the baby farm or could be the culprit and had come there to kill them. To permanently silence them in case they'd learned anything while undercover.

"I'll come to you," Austin finally said. "But first tell me what you have. I want to make sure it's worth risking my neck."

"Oh, it's worth the risk, all right. But it'll cost you. I need money to get away from here, and I figure the McKinnons have plenty of it."

Blackmail. That turned Rosalie's stomach, but if she were in Vickie's shoes, she might be forced to consider doing the same thing.

"How much do you want?" Rosalie asked.

"Ten grand."

Rosalie didn't know the financial workings of the ranch, but she knew it was very successful, and it was highly likely that there was at least that much or more in the safe in Roy's office.

"I'll call the main house," Rosalie whispered to Austin, but he caught on to her hand to stop her.

"I'm not just walking down to you, carrying ten grand," Austin said to Vickie. "You need to tell me what you have."

Silence. For a long time. So long that Rosalie's heartbeat started to throb in her ears. If the woman refused and just drove away, the information might be lost. Still, there was Austin's safety to consider. Rosalie definitely didn't want him out there if this could turn into another attack.

"Well?" Austin prompted.

"The man who brought me your nephew called himself Jack Smith," Vickie finally said. "There was a woman with him, dressed in white scrubs like a nurse. Anyway, the baby had some kind of seeds on his blanket."

"Seeds?" Austin and Rosalie asked in unison. That certainly wasn't something Rosalie expected Vickie to say.

"I mean the baby was clean and everything except for those seeds. I asked about them. More like casual conversation, you know, and the woman said they'd picked up the baby at the grain mill about ten miles from where I lived. Smith shushed her right up, and told me that the birth mother had hidden the pregnancy from her parents, and that she met them there at the mill so her folks wouldn't find out that she'd given birth."

"And you believed Smith?" Austin pressed.

"I did at the time. I didn't think anything more about it until after this mess with the baby farm broke loose. Then, I began to think it might be a ruse of some kind. I mean, why would the birth mother choose to meet them in a grain mill?"

"You mean the old abandoned one on the other side of town?" Rosalie had only vague memories of the silo that jutted up in an overgrown field.

"That's the one," Vickie verified. "It's exactly ten miles from me just like the woman said, and there's not another one in the area. I went over there last night, looking for answers."

"You did what?" Austin cursed again.

"I didn't go alone. I took a couple of friends with me. They were armed, but the guns weren't needed. Nobody was there. Just some boxes with files in them." Vickie paused. "The files are connected to the baby farm."

"Files," Austin snapped, not sounding at all happy about this. "You contaminated a scene that could be critical to this investigation."

"I found proof of the person who got Rosalie McKinnon's daughter," Vickie insisted. "And if you want it, it'll cost you ten grand. I'll be waiting at the end of the road."

"Meet me at the sheriff's office," Austin argued, but he was talking to himself because Vickie had already ended the call.

Austin jabbed the button to return the call. No answer. It went straight to voice mail.

"I'll see about getting the money," Rosalie said, hurrying to the landline in the kitchen.

She considered calling her sister, who was still staying in the main house with her fiancé, but Rayanne was pregnant, and Rosalie didn't want her anywhere near Vickie or the danger. Her brother Cooper was at his own house, which was about a quarter of a mile away. Not far, but it would eat up precious moments if he was the one she involved in this. Ditto for her other brother Tucker.

That left her younger brother, Colt, and her father.

Rosalie pressed in the number, not sure which she would get, and it was Colt who answered on the first ring.

"What the hell's going on?" Colt immediately said. "The ranch hands just called, and there's a woman parked right in front of the gate—"

"I need ten thousand in cash," Rosalie interrupted. "The woman says she has information about my daughter."

Rosalie took a deep breath, praying that whatever files Vickie had would do just that—help her find Sadie—and that it would all happen without anyone else getting hurt.

"I'll be right there," Colt assured her before she could tell him that she'd pay him back as soon as she could get to the bank.

Like Vickie, Colt quickly ended the call, and Rosalie hurried back to the front of the cottage to see what was going on. Austin was already outside on the porch, his gun drawn and his attention on the small black car at the end of the road.

"Stay back," he warned her.

Rosalie did, but it was hard to do that with possible answers this close. It seemed to take an eternity, but she realized it was less than five minutes before Colt emerged from the main house and headed toward them. He, too, was carrying a gun and a thick plastic bag.

Austin turned around, snagged her gaze and slipped his cell into his shirt pocket. "Wait here, and I mean it. Don't you even think about going out there with me. Call me, and I'll leave my phone on so you can hear what's going on."

She nodded, her breath hitching a little when he idly brushed a kiss on her mouth and headed out, Colt falling in step right along beside him. As Austin had instructed, she called him, but he didn't speak when he answered the call. Probably because he wanted to keep his attention on the woman who stepped from the car.

It was Vickie all right.

The woman had a large cardboard box that she set on the ground next to the fence, and she took out a manila folder from it.

"I want the money," Vickie said when Austin and Colt approached her. "Then, you'll get the files."

"Show me that folder first," Austin countered.

Because his back was to her, Rosalie couldn't see Austin's expression, but it must have been adamant enough for Vickie to rethink her demand. She handed him the folder.

Colt kept his gun trained on the woman while

he volleyed glances at both Austin and the folder he opened. Time seemed to stop. Not her heart, though. It was slamming against her chest so hard that it hurt her ribs.

"Give her the cash," Austin finally said. He glanced back over his shoulder at Rosalie. "Judging from the birthday, this could be Sadie's file."

Rosalie sucked in her breath so hard that she nearly got choked. "And?" was all she managed to say.

She heard Austin's hard breath, too, but it was Vickie who answered. "Tell Rosalie that it has the name of the person who bought her daughter."

Chapter Twelve

Austin wished like the devil that he could stop Rosalie from going with him for this visit, but he knew he didn't stand a chance of making her stay at her family's ranch. One way or another she would confront the man whose name had been in the file that Vickie had given them.

Trevor Yancy.

Austin shouldn't have been surprised to see Yancy's name on those papers claiming he was the one who'd *bought* Sadie. After all, the man was a serious suspect in the baby farm investigation and a multitude of other felonies. However, just the fact that it was Yancy meant that Rosalie wasn't going to settle for anyone but her confronting him.

He couldn't blame her.

But Austin darn sure could do whatever it took to protect her.

That's why he was driving her to Yancy's estate in San Antonio while her brother Colt followed them in his truck. In addition, Austin had called SAPD and asked them to send out a patrol car to keep an eye on the estate, to make sure Yancy didn't try to run. Maybe, just maybe, Yancy would confess to everything, turn over a perfectly healthy Sadie to Rosalie and then Colt could arrest the piece of slime.

Austin only hoped Rosalie and he could keep their own tempers in check during this little chat.

He had a lot of dangerous energy brewing inside him, and that anger was headed right toward Yancy. The man had likely caused Eli's death, and now he might have been the one to kidnap Rosalie's daughter.

If Yancy had done that, he was going to pay hard.

"Hurry," she insisted.

Rosalie kept her attention on the phone, and pressed Redial yet again. As with the other half dozen times that she'd tried to call Yancy on both his cell and home phones, the man didn't answer. Maybe because he didn't take calls this early or maybe because Vickie or someone else had given him a heads-up that Rosalie and the law were on the way. Of course, Austin wasn't sure why Vickie would do something like that since she'd been the one to give them the file, but with all the insanity that'd gone on, anything was possible.

"If Yancy's not home, we'll find him," Austin promised her, and it was a promise he would keep no matter what it took. Too bad though that he couldn't keep it after he had Rosalie tucked safely away. He hadn't stopped her from going to the estate, but if this turned into an all-out search, he wanted her far away from any path that Yancy and his hired thugs might take.

"I want to hear what he has to say about those adoption papers," Rosalie mumbled.

"So do I. But if he does actually answer your call, it's best not to ask him if he has Sadie. We wouldn't want to spook him and have him run with her."

"I doubt he can be spooked. He's arrogant and certain that he's above the law. He's not."

No, he wasn't. "But until we have Yancy in our sights, it's best if you keep the adoption questions general. Don't ask specifically about Sadie. Agreed?"

He could tell she wanted to argue with him about that, but she finally nodded.

Her grip tightened even more on the phone until Austin thought it might shatter. Heck, she might shatter, too. Not with tears this time, but he could feel the rage boiling inside her just as it was with him.

"You have to remember that Vickie or someone else could have faked that paperwork," Austin reminded her.

The anger flashed in her eyes as if she might argue about that, as well, but then a rough groan left her mouth. "I know. Vickie could be lying to cover her own guilt."

Yeah, and that's the reason Austin had called Rosalie's brother, the sheriff, so he could escort Vickie into town for questioning. Vickie hadn't liked that one bit, but Austin didn't care. She'd possibly destroyed evidence by going to that grain mill.

And maybe worse.

"Maybe Vickie pretended to go to the grain mill to cover up any DNA evidence that might be there. *Her* DNA," Austin clarified.

Rosalie made a sound of agreement. "But if she's guilty, why didn't she stay hidden away? She's the one who contacted us about your nephew. Vickie could have just stayed in hiding or given the baby to someone else so that she wouldn't be caught with him."

Unfortunately, Austin could see that from another angle. "She could have heard that I'd been working undercover to find Nathan and thought she'd better cut her losses. By giving him to us, she might have hoped to get the heat off her and put it on someone else."

"And she could have used the files to set up Yancy," Rosalie finished for him a moment later. "That would explain why she didn't just blow up the grain mill." Her eyes narrowed. "That doesn't mean Yancy's innocent, though."

No, it didn't. But with all the finger-pointing that Sonny, Vickie and Yancy were doing at each other, it was hard to home in on the guilty party.

Rosalie tried Yancy's number again. Same result. No answer. She checked the estimated time of arrival on the GPS. Yet something else she'd been doing since they started this drive from the McKinnon ranch. They were still a half hour out, and that likely felt like an eternity to her.

It did to Austin, too.

It also didn't help that they were in the middle of a long stretch of rural property.

He'd taken the back roads to get there as fast as possible, but it meant Rosalie, Colt and he were at risk for another attack. The rural road would be a good place for it. Of course, the gunmen could have come after them on the highway, too. No place would be truly safe until the men were found and put in jail along with their boss.

And maybe their boss was Yancy.

"If Yancy has Sadie—"

"Don't go there," he insisted.

Austin hooked his arm around her and

dragged her as close to him as the seat belt would allow. It wasn't exactly a hug to comfort her, but it was the best he could do. He definitely didn't want her to think about why Yancy would have purchased her child.

Because nothing good came to mind.

There was no acceptable reason for a weasel like Yancy to buy a baby.

That sent a new round of rage through him. If Yancy had done anything to Sadie, then no way would Austin be able to keep his temper in check. He would aim every bit of his venom at the man.

"I'm trying Yancy's cell again." Rosalie pressed Redial again, and Austin was about to tell her that she should just wait until they got to his place. But this time, she didn't get his voice mail.

Yancy answered.

"It's early," Yancy snarled. "What in Sam Hill do you want at this hour?"

Probably because she was so shocked that he'd actually picked up, it took Rosalie a moment to find her voice. Or maybe she was remembering all the things that Austin had warned her that she shouldn't say to him.

"What do you really know about the baby farms?" she asked.

Yancy cursed. "Not this again. I'm getting sick and tired of these—"

"Did you try to adopt a baby?" Rosalie snapped.

Austin held his breath, wondering if it might not be a good idea, after all, to go ahead and try to spook Yancy. The SAPD patrol was hopefully already in place at his house so they could stop the man from fleeing. And if Yancy did indeed run, it would just confirm his guilt.

"Who the devil told you that?" Yancy asked.

"Just answer the question," Austin insisted, using his lawman's tone that no doubt set Yancy's teeth on edge. "Did you have anything to do with trying to adopt a baby?"

"Yeah," Yancy finally said after mumbling plenty of profanity. "About a year ago, but I didn't go through with it. The only reason I wanted a kid was to keep my wife happy so she wouldn't divorce me and take a fortune. She decided to leave me, anyway, so I canceled the adoption."

Rosalie glanced at Austin to see if he was buying this, but he had to shrug. It sounded exactly like something Yancy would do, and Yancy had been through a bitter divorce. From what Austin remembered, there'd been no prenup, and Yancy's ex-wife had gotten millions from his estate.

Still, that didn't mean Yancy hadn't taken Rosalie's daughter.

"You have any proof that you backed out of the deal?" Rosalie asked.

A few long moments crawled by. "You got proof that I didn't?"

"Yes, I think we do."

Yancy's next round of profanity was significantly worse. "I told you I had no part in that business with the baby farms, and if you've got something that says different, then it's a lie just like the ones Sonny-boy was spewing."

"You're sure?" Austin pressed, causing Yancy's profanity to continue.

"Damn straight. And ask yourself this little question. Why would an operation like this keep records lying around for someone to find? They wouldn't. So, anything you find or will find has been manufactured to make somebody look guilty. And in this case, that manufacturing has been aimed at me."

Yancy had a point, but it was a point all three suspects could make. There was situational evidence to suggest that all of them had motive and opportunity to pull off an operation like this. Sonny and Yancy had the means with their bank accounts, and Austin was sure if he dug harder, that he'd find Vickie had those same means.

"If you're telling the truth," Rosalie said,

obviously ignoring his question, "then you won't mind if we search your house."

"Heck, yeah, I mind—"

Yancy continued to talk, but Austin tuned him out. That's because he saw the large SUV coming down the road toward them, and it looked like the vehicle their attackers had used. Not a good time for this to happen since Austin was approaching a bridge where there'd be no place to maneuver.

He moved his hand over his gun and was about to call Colt to alert him, but the SUV swerved directly into their lane.

And it came right at them.

ROSALIE HAD HER attention focused on Yancy's rant so it took her a moment to realize that something was wrong.

Oh, God.

It was happening again. They were in danger.

"Hold on!" Austin shouted a split second before he jerked the steering wheel to the right. If he hadn't done that, the SUV would have crashed right into them.

Instead, their front bumper bashed into the concrete guardrail on the narrow bridge. Her body jolted forward only to be slammed back again when the air bags deployed and hit her right in the face.

She couldn't see, but mercy, she could feel. The impact knocked the breath right out of her. Thankfully, though, Austin seemed to be able to react. He quickly batted down the deflating air bag on his side because the truck was still moving. And Rosalie got a glimpse of where they were headed.

Straight down the bank and into the creek.

Austin fought the steering wheel, and he hit the brakes. But it was already too late. Rosalie put up her hands to brace herself for the impact.

She didn't have to wait long.

It seemed only a blink of an eye before the truck plowed right into the water. The impact gave her body another jolt, knocking her off balance. Before she could even get the door open, icy water started pouring into the cab.

"Colt's behind us," Austin mumbled.

Maybe he said that so she wouldn't panic and would remember that they had backup. However, her brother could be under attack, as well.

Rosalie frantically tried to open the door, and her heart skipped a beat when it didn't budge. Neither did Austin's, but he slammed his shoulder against it until it gave way, and he pried it the rest of the way open with his hands.

"Come on," he said, keeping his gun and phone above the water that was rushing in.

He caught on to her wrist and pulled her closer

toward him. However, he didn't get out. Austin looked up at the SUV, probably to make sure they weren't about to be gunned down when they exited the vehicle.

"They're still out there on the bridge," Austin told her. "Keep low and move fast."

That didn't help steady her heart, and she was already shaking so hard that Rosalie was afraid she wouldn't be able to move. Austin made sure she did, though. With the water inside the truck already chest high and getting deeper, he pulled her into the creek.

The water wasn't over their heads, but it was freezing, and the cold blasted through her. Her teeth started to chatter and she was shaking. Still, Austin kept her moving. Not toward the gunmen and Colt but toward the bank on the opposite side of the creek.

Her heartbeat was so loud in her ears, and with the water raging around them, it took Rosalie a moment to realize some of what she was hearing were gunshots.

Sweet heaven.

Not again.

They were under attack and literally out in the open. Plus, her brother was no doubt being shot at, too. Hopefully, Colt had managed to stay safe and could return fire.

Somehow, Austin was able to keep his gun

and phone out of the water while he also kept her moving. Her heart was pounding even harder, her breath barely there by the time they made it to the bank. It was a mixture of dead grass, icy mud and rocks, and they crawled toward one of the large boulders. With her wet clothes weighing her down, each inch was a challenge.

The moment that Austin got her behind the boulder, he turned and fired at the people shooting at them. Rosalie got a glimpse of the men then. Both had taken cover behind their SUV. One had his weapon aimed at them. The other had his aimed in the direction of Colt's truck. She didn't see her brother, but she heard the sound of the gunshots coming from his direction.

Thank God.

Maybe Colt would be able to capture at least one of the men so that Austin and she could finally get some answers as to what was going on. However, she wasn't sure it was a coincidence that they'd been attacked so close to Yancy's house.

Was Yancy trying to kill them so she wouldn't find her daughter?

That only made her anger and resolve stronger, and Rosalie wished she'd managed to hang on to a gun so that she could help Austin and Colt return fire.

"Backup's on the way!" Colt shouted to them.

Rosalie didn't know if that was a bluff or if Colt had actually managed to make a call with all the chaos going on around them. Either way, it stopped the men from shooting, and she saw one of them motion toward the other.

The pair hurried to get back inside their SUV.

Oh, mercy. "They can't get away," Rosalie whispered. Even though she didn't want more bullets coming toward them or Colt, she also didn't want them to escape. Obviously, neither did Austin.

Cursing, he levered himself up, took aim and fired a shot at the man getting behind the steering wheel. His first shot missed.

His second didn't.

Rosalie saw the man's shoulder snap back, and he howled in pain. However, it didn't stop him. He jumped into the driver's seat and slammed the door shut. His partner did the same on the other side of the SUV.

Both Colt and Austin didn't stop shooting. Austin came out from behind the boulder, and standing, he fired directly at the driver again. The bullet tore into the glass, shattering it.

Just as the driver jammed on the accelerator.

Even if he was hurt and bleeding, he was still managing to get away.

The SUV flew past Colt's truck, barely missing her brother.

"Come on," Austin said, pulling Rosalie to her feet.

She wasn't sure how he managed to move so fast as they hurried back into the creek and toward the bank. While still keeping watch around them, Colt barreled down the slick incline to help them. The moment they made it back out of the water, the three of them raced toward his truck.

"Are you hurt?" Colt asked.

Austin gave her a quick once-over and shook his head. "Hurry," he told Colt. "We have to find those gunmen."

Colt didn't waste another second. He gunned the engine, and they went in pursuit.

Chapter Thirteen

Austin looked at the purple bruise on Rosalie's cheek and cursed again. He had no idea when she'd gotten it, but it'd probably happened when they'd plunged into the creek.

Where they could have died.

He was responsible for that. He should have done everything to stop her from going to Yancy's estate, should have forced her to let him protect her. But he hadn't, and she'd paid another high price for it.

"I must look pretty bad, huh?" Rosalie mumbled.

She had another sip of the hot tea that one of the Sweetwater Springs deputies had fixed for her. In addition to the tea sipping, she was also pacing back and forth in front of the doorway of the sheriff's office.

Since she was still shivering a little from the adrenaline crash, the hot tea obviously wasn't doing its job. Ditto for the change of dry clothes that her brother had brought for both Austin and her from the ranch. Of course, tea and dry clothes weren't nearly enough to erase the nightmarish memories from this latest attack.

Or erase the fact that their attackers had gotten away again.

The men were out there, no doubt ready to come after them the first chance they got. It was up to Austin to make sure another chance was the last thing they got.

"You look fine," Austin assured her.

She made a *yeah, right* sound and paused her pacing so she could glance out into the squad room. The place was cluttered with cops, two of them her own brothers. Her other brother, Tucker, a Texas Ranger, was also there. All of them were on the phone. All trying to track down those gunmen and deal with the Yancy situation.

Obviously, no one had made any headway or they would have come into the sheriff's office, where Rosalie and Austin were waiting for news.

Any news.

But especially news that concerned the search warrant they'd managed to get for Yancy's place. With luck, there'd soon be a team of cops and FBI agents, including Seth, streaming through the house and grounds to look for any shred of evidence.

With even better luck, they'd find Sadie.

Of course, Yancy's place wasn't the only lead they had. Austin was sure he'd wounded one of their attackers. Colt had possibly wounded the other. It meant the men would have to get medical attention, and maybe they'd do that at a hospital where their injuries would be reported. Then, once they had the gunmen in custody, it would make it easier to find out who'd hired them.

Austin hoped so, anyway.

Sooner or later they had to catch a break that didn't end in them nearly being killed.

"I don't know if I can stand around here waiting much longer," Rosalie said, gripping the cup of tea so hard that her knuckles were turning white.

Yeah, he felt the same way, and yet Austin knew there was little more that they could do. Well, other than take Rosalie back to her family's ranch.

Something she'd repeatedly refused.

Austin couldn't blame her.

Since she couldn't be at Yancy's house while it was being searched, the sheriff's office was the next best place. At least they'd be there when Yancy was brought in, and there was no doubt about it—the man would be brought in for questioning.

As a minimum, Yancy had to answer questions about the files that Vickie had given them. Of course, he'd lie about them, but with the photos from Sonny and now the files, that might be enough to make an arrest. Being tossed behind bars might get Yancy to bargain with them, and he could just open up about Sadie and anything that he might actually know about her.

Eleven months was a long time to hold a child, and that meant there might be records for payment of nannies and baby supplies. Well, there would be if Yancy hadn't simply given her away to someone. But maybe there'd be something in his house about that, too. Yes, Yancy was careful, always covering his tracks, but maybe he'd gotten sloppy about this.

"I wish you'd see a medic," Austin tried again when he gave that angry-looking bruise another glance. Perhaps this time, she would actually agree.

But Rosalie only shook her head and touched her fingers to the wound on her face that kept snagging his attention. "It's not bad. I'm okay."

"You're not okay. You're still shaking." Austin stood, went to her and pried the cup from her hands so he could set it on the desk.

"It's not a good time for you to hold me," Rosalie protested.

That was yet something else they could agree

on, but it didn't stop Austin from pulling her into his arms because she looked as if she needed it.

Heck, who was he kidding?

He needed it, too. Needed to feel her next to him. Needed the way she sort of melted against him. He got it all right. But it came at a high cost—it only made him need her more. And it broke down even more of those barriers that she kept putting up between them.

Rosalie eased back, just a little, meeting him eye to eye. That wasn't a happy expression on her face. "We keep getting closer and closer."

Austin figured his expression wasn't happy, either. "I want you," he settled for saying. "So yeah, we're getting closer."

Rosalie stared at him a long time, as if trying to figure out a way to dismiss what he'd just admitted, but then she huffed. Her breath from that huff was still on his mouth when she kissed him. She didn't settle for a peck but instead turned it into the kind of kiss that he knew they should be avoiding.

Oh, man.

He was just plain brainless when it came to Rosalie, and Austin proved that by kissing her right back. The timing sucked. Same for the location. But did that stop him?

Nope.

He kept it up until both of them were in serious need of some air. Or maybe a bed.

"I'm not sure I'm ready for this," she said, her mouth still way too close to his. "And it could be that I'm just using this right now, using *you,* to get my mind off Sadie."

Since it was the equivalent of a *no,* that got him backing away. Or rather it would have if Rosalie hadn't caught on to the front of his shirt to anchor him in place.

"But I don't think I can stop myself, either," Rosalie added. "And maybe I'm not using you at all. Maybe I just…want you."

Since that was pretty much the equivalent of a big green light, Austin went after her again, and he could have stood there kissing her for hours if he hadn't heard the footsteps headed in their direction. He broke away from her just as Colt stepped into the doorway.

Rosalie's brother wasn't an idiot, and his lifted eyebrow let Austin know that he knew what was going on. But that raised eyebrow lasted only a second before Colt motioned for them to follow him.

"The team's out at Yancy's place," Colt explained as they made their way to a desk in the corner of the squad room. "Yancy's not there, but the team entered the premises, and one of the

SAPD officers is recording the search. Thought you'd like to watch on the computer."

That was a massive understatement, and Rosalie practically ran to the laptop centered on the desk. Sure enough, it was the front door of Yancy's place. Austin had been there at least a half dozen times when questioning the man about various investigations, including the one leading up to Eli's murder.

The officer filming the search walked into the massive marble foyer, where a maid was waiting and glaring. Obviously, she wasn't pleased about this intrusion, but she didn't try to stop them.

"The maid said no one else was home," Colt explained.

"What about a baby?" Rosalie asked.

Colt shook his head. "It was the first thing Seth asked her, and she claims a baby's never lived at the estate, and she's worked there for ten years."

Austin could practically feel the disappointment ripple through her. And the relief.

"The maid's on Yancy's payroll," Austin reminded her. "Judging from her expression, she's loyal to him, which means she'd lie to protect him."

Yeah, that was bittersweet, too, because if the woman was indeed lying, they might find Sadie today. In Yancy's house. But it would mean the monster had had Rosalie's precious baby all this time. Since that only caused Austin's blood to boil, he tried to push the possibility aside. Best to wait and see how this all panned out.

Best-case scenario was for the cops to find Sadie's file and for Rosalie to learn that her baby had been adopted by a loving family. Illegally adopted, that is. Then, Rosalie could petition for the baby's return once she'd done the DNA tests. It wouldn't be a simple process, but this search could give them a start.

The cop with the camera moved past the maid and into the adjoining living room, where another officer was going through a cluttered bookshelf. Austin watched as the cameraman made his way to the side of the house and to Yancy's office.

"There's Seth," Rosalie mumbled when her brother came into view. The camera was filming him while he was at Yancy's desk going through the drawers.

Rosalie automatically reached for her phone, no doubt to call her brother, but then she groaned when she realized that she'd lost it in the creek. Instead, she snatched up the one on the desk, pressed in his number, and a moment later Austin saw Seth answer the call.

"Seth—" Rosalie said.

"We haven't found anything," Seth immediately interrupted, glancing up at the camera as if to make eye contact with his sister.

"Where's Yancy?" Austin asked, and he pressed the button to put the call on speaker.

"There was no sign of him when we arrived. The maid says he's away on business, but she could be lying. We've got the airports covered and a BOLO on his vehicles."

Rosalie shook her head. "Yancy might be on the run."

But something wasn't right about that. Yancy wasn't a runner. He'd come close to arrest many times and had always relied on his team of high-priced lawyers to keep his butt out of jail.

Maybe this was something his lawyers couldn't fix.

Like his guilt over running a baby farm. The baby farm could net him murder charges along with other assorted felonies.

There was some chatter outside Yancy's office, and Seth got up to check it out. Thankfully, the officer with the camera followed Rosalie's brother out into the hall and to the bottom of a massive curved staircase.

"You need to get a look at this," a uniformed cop told Seth.

"It's not what you think," the maid shouted, following right along behind them as they hurried up the stairs.

Oh, man. What the heck had they found?

Since Rosalie suddenly didn't look too steady on her feet, Austin slipped his arm around her waist. They didn't have to wait long to see what was happening.

The camera soon picked up the officer standing outside a room at the far end of the hall. Beside him, Rosalie pulled in her breath, and they watched together. The officer in the doorway stepped aside so that Seth and the cameraman could get a look.

"Oh, God," Rosalie said, her hand flying to her mouth.

Austin repeated it.

Because it was a nursery. And not just any old nursery. This one was drenched in pink. The walls, the bed, the toys.

Everything for a baby girl.

"It's not what you think!" the maid repeated, and she tried to shoulder Seth and the cameraman aside. That didn't work. And the glare that Seth gave her could have frozen Hades a couple of times over.

"Where's the baby?" Seth demanded.

The maid frantically shook her head. "There's no baby. Never was. Mrs. Yancy had this room set up because they planned to adopt a baby, but the adoption didn't go through because they got a divorce."

That meshed with what Yancy had told them, but Austin wasn't about to believe Yancy or his maid. Apparently, neither was Seth. He went into the room, looking around for what seemed an eternity.

"It doesn't look as if the crib or the room has been used," he finally said after a heavy sigh. "Rosalie, I don't think Sadie was here."

Again, Austin could see the conflict of emotions on her face, and it was a good thing he was holding on to her because she practically sagged against him.

"Just in case, I'll have the CSI team process the room," Seth continued. "We might find something. Might find something on his computers, too, because I'm confiscating all of them along with the files in his office."

Good. Maybe Yancy had left something incriminating behind. Austin could hope so, anyway. The minutes were just ticking away, and if they hoped to have Sadie home by Christmas, then…

Austin mentally stopped.

Home.

Not his home, either, but Rosalie's. It would be an incredible reunion, one that he would do whatever it took to make sure it happened. But after that, Rosalie and Sadie would be out of his life. Without the danger, there'd be no excuse for him to stay around. Yes, the attraction was there between Rosalie and him.

But there was also the doubt.

Maybe once she had Sadie, the doubt would be more than enough for Rosalie to tell him to take a hike. That sure didn't settle well in his stomach or any other part of him.

"Is something wrong?" he heard Rosalie ask, and it took Austin a moment to realize she was talking to him and that there was a concerned look on her face.

Great. He didn't want to add to her troubles, so he shook his head. "Just thinking."

And wondering how stupid he had to be to fall for a woman who wasn't ready to fall again. Especially not for him. The bad memories would always be there, and he wasn't sure the bad ones would ever outshine the good ones.

"We got a visitor," one of the officers told Seth. That got Austin's attention back where it belonged. On the search going on at Yancy's estate.

The cameraman continued to get footage of every nook and cranny of the nursery, but Seth stepped out of the room and out of camera range.

"Sonny's here," Seth told them, and he motioned for the cameraman to film what could easily turn into another encounter. Sonny seemed to bring trouble with him wherever he went.

It wasn't long before Austin heard the man's thundering voice. "Where the hell is he?" Sonny demanded.

Sonny was coming up the hall toward Seth and moving a lot easier than he had the last time Austin had seen him, but he was just as riled as he had been when he'd pulled a gun on Yancy at the hospital.

"I have no idea. I was hoping you could tell me where Yancy is," Seth countered.

"Well, I can't," Sonny snapped, but he held up an envelope for Seth. "But he's trying to set me up again."

"Funny, Yancy keeps saying the same thing about you." Seth took the envelope that Sonny practically slapped into his hand.

The camera angle was bad and Austin couldn't see what Seth took from the envelope, but it appeared to be photos.

Seth studied them for several long moments, and the cameraman finally moved in on the image.

A baby.

"Who is this?" Seth demanded.

"Read the memo." Sonny rifled through the eight-by-ten black-and-white photos to what appeared to be a single paragraph.

Seth did read it. Too bad Austin couldn't do the same, but whatever was on the page caused

Seth to pull back his shoulders. "Where the hell did you get this?" His gaze snapped to Sonny.

"Someone broke into my office and put it in one of my files. I'm sure they did that for you to find so you'd arrest me."

A soft gasp left Rosalie's mouth. "Is it Sadie?" But she didn't wait for Seth or Sonny to answer. "Let me see the photos. Hold them up to the camera."

Austin hadn't seen a photo of Sadie, but he could tell from Rosalie's reaction that this was indeed her baby. It was a snapshot of a newborn baby sleeping in a carried seat.

Rosalie moved as if to bolt to the door. No doubt to go see the photos for herself, but Austin stopped her.

"Don't come here," Seth warned her. Even though he couldn't see his sister, he must have known what her reaction would be.

Every muscle in her body was tight now, but she cursed and stayed put. "Show me the rest of the photos."

Seth did after he, too, mumbled some profanity. The next picture was also of Sadie in the arms of a woman. The camera was on the baby, not the person holding her, so Austin could see the little girl's blond hair and a round baby face.

"Who's that woman with her?" Rosalie

demanded, and Seth repeated the question to Sonny.

"I don't know." No shout from Sonny this time. He scrubbed his hand over his face and appeared to be in as much shock over this as they were. "Like I said, someone planted the photos in my office. But I'm guessing that she's a nanny."

Probably, and she appeared to be taking good care of the baby. That was something at least. But Austin wanted more—the woman's identity and where the picture was taken.

Maybe Seth could get those answers from Sonny.

Seth went to the next photo. No newborn this time, but Austin was pretty sure it was Sadie. The little girl was about four or five months old, lying in a crib and smiling from ear to ear, kicking her arms and legs as she looked up at the person who'd taken her picture.

Austin tightened his grip on Rosalie when she wobbled again. She finally sank into the chair, her attention nailed to the laptop screen and her trembling fingers pressed to her mouth.

"That next picture's been photoshopped," Sonny insisted. "It had to have been."

Rosalie moved closer to the screen, but Seth turned away so that he got a look at the photo first. No doubt so he could try to shelter his sister in case it was something he didn't want her to see.

Seth cursed. It wasn't mumbled this time, either.

"Show it to me!" Rosalie demanded just as Sonny repeated, "It's a fake."

"I'll have the lab check and make sure it's real," Seth told her. "It has a date stamp on it that says it was taken three days ago." He finally held the photo up for Rosalie to see.

She gasped.

The photo was of a little girl, blond curls haloing around her head. She was smiling in this snapshot, too, and looking up at the woman who was lovingly holding her in her arms.

And that woman was Vickie.

Chapter Fourteen

Everything inside her felt as if she was spinning out of control, but Rosalie tried to hang on to her sanity. Especially since Seth, Austin and even Sonny had reminded her that the photos could have been doctored.

Still, that was her baby in the pictures. Rosalie was sure of it.

She sat at the kitchen table and studied the copies of the photos that Seth had faxed to the ranch guesthouse. Probably a ploy to make sure she stayed put with Austin while the cops looked for Vickie and Yancy. It was working.

For now.

But with this pressure cooker of emotions building inside her, she couldn't spend days or even hours waiting for answers from two people who had seemingly disappeared.

Austin was on the phone, pacing the guest cottage living room, but he also kept his eye on her. Something he'd been doing a lot since they'd arrived about an hour earlier. Like Seth, Austin was afraid she'd go stark raving mad and run out the door.

The probability for that was fairly high.

She ran her fingertips over the photo that according to the time-date stamp been taken only days earlier. Rosalie touched the image of her baby's hair. Her face. There were so many features that she recognized. The shape of Sadie's face was like her own. Ditto for the hair. Rosalie had seen photos of herself as a child, and her own hair was exactly like the cloud of curls.

But that was Eli's smile.

It broke her heart and warmed her all at the same time. A part of him had lived on. Too bad Rosalie hadn't been able to experience it firsthand.

God, she'd missed so much.

Eleven months was a lifetime to be apart from her child.

Rosalie's heart was broken over that. And the pain crushed her chest so that it felt as if someone had put her entire body in a vise. Squeezing and choking her until the panic attack started to crawl through her again.

Rosalie threw back the chair, got up and headed for the door. She needed some fresh air. Needed to run. To scream. To do something to stop the torture. A panic attack wouldn't do anyone any good, and it would only cause Austin and Seth to worry about her even more.

If that was possible.

"The guards from the baby farm," Austin reminded her. He stepped in front of her just as she opened the door. "If you go outside, they could use long-range rifles to shoot at you."

He locked the door, set the security system, eased his arm around her and tried to maneuver her into the living room. But Rosalie held her ground. She couldn't sit down a moment longer.

"Give me some good news," she begged. "Please."

Judging from the length of time it took him to answer, he was clearly having trouble coming up with something. "The photos are top priority for the lab, so we should know within an hour or two if they're fake."

"They're not fake." Then, she shook her head. "The baby is real. It's Sadie. *My* baby. But it's possible that Vickie's image was doctored in."

Or not.

It sickened her even more to think of Vickie having had Sadie all this time. Of course, there were worse alternatives.

Like Yancy or Sonny.

Of the three, Vickie seemed the safest choice, but if she'd lied so easily to their faces, then heaven knew what she was capable of doing to a baby.

"The cops and the FBI are working this hard," Austin reminded her. "And Seth will make sure there are no delays." No doubt a second attempt to give her some more good news.

Yes, it was good, but it didn't seem nearly enough. Though it would never happen, she wanted every law enforcement agency in the state on this.

"You should sit back down," he said.

This time when he urged her into the living room, she went, but she stopped first to grab the photos. She dropped them on the coffee table so she could look at them when they sat on the sofa.

"Someone has her," Rosalie mumbled. "Seth and the others have to find out who that is."

"They will. They're looking for Vickie and Yancy right now," Austin assured her. "And Seth will call the moment he finds out anything. If the lab can identify where the photos of Sadie were taken, then we can get a search warrant."

Yes, her mind knew that, but that didn't make this situation more bearable.

"You don't have to keep yourself together for my sake," Austin added. "If you need to lose it, then go ahead. Scream, curse, kick, do whatever will help."

"Kick?" she questioned.

The corner of his mouth lifted a little. "I was hoping you'd go for one of the other choices, but my shins are ready if you need to kick something."

"If I thought for one minute it'd help, I might try it." She paused, and though she hadn't intended for her gaze to go in that direction, she eyed the front of his jeans. "Just not your shins, though."

He feigned a wince. "Okay, but please don't aim *there*."

Rosalie didn't laugh, but it did ease the tension a bit. Something she hadn't thought possible just moments earlier. Leave it to Austin to work some magic and lighten her mood.

"Sit," he suggested. "Breathe." His voice was smoky deep now, like a smooth shot of whiskey. It was void of all the raw emotion they'd been through in the past couple of days.

Rosalie didn't sit, but his suggestion caused her to calm down enough so that she could study the photos again. Yes, she'd already studied them until her eyes were burning, but this time she noticed something obvious that she'd missed.

There wasn't much background in the shots of Sadie, but in all three cases, it appeared to be the same room. Not a dingy holding cell, either, but rather a cheerful-looking nursery. Exactly the kind of room she'd set up for her baby at her house in Kendall County.

"Maybe the person who adopted her didn't know she'd been stolen," Rosalie said. Maybe this person holding her baby wasn't the monster she was making the individual out to be but rather a loving parent who'd desperately wanted a child.

That thought helped. Some.

So did the way that Austin pulled her deeper into the curve of his arm. Yet something else that was smooth and comforting. It was dangerous for her to get so close to him right now, but Rosalie didn't care. Austin understood what she was going through.

He understood *her*.

And right now, the curve of his arm felt like the right place to be. Sadly, this was more than just a comforting gesture, though. His arms were a place where she could shut out these painful memories and find comfort of a different nature.

She turned to face him. Also dangerous. But she wanted to kiss him. Wanted to feel something other than this dark storm that had hemmed her in like a straitjacket.

And she felt *something* all right.

One touch of his mouth to hers, and she got a quick reminder of why this wasn't a very good idea. The dark storm vanished, but in its place came a storm of a different kind. A fiery-hot one that threatened to burn them alive.

A sound of surprise rumbled deep in his throat. Rosalie heard the question there, too.

Is this a good idea?

It wasn't.

But that didn't stop her.

She slid her hand around the back of his neck, bringing him closer so she could lose herself in the kiss. Lose herself in his touch. In Austin.

He automatically adjusted, turning, so he could gather her in his arms and deepen the kiss.

Yes!

This was the fire that she wanted. *Needed.* And Rosalie would have done her own share of kiss-deepening if Austin hadn't pulled back.

Their breaths were already gusting, and she could feel the urgency in her body. Still, he held her back from him, his gaze meeting hers.

"Think this through. Be sure it's what you want," Austin said, obviously giving her an out.

Rosalie did think about it. Well, as best as she could, considering the kiss had done its job of clouding her thoughts and common sense. Or maybe Austin alone was responsible. Either way, she didn't have to think long.

Even if she regretted it, she was going to be with him.

And Rosalie let Austin know that by pulling him back to her.

AUSTIN DIDN'T FEEL any hesitation from Rosalie. Just the opposite. But he had to wonder—was this about him, or did she just need him for a distraction?

He didn't know the answer. Wasn't sure that Rosalie did, either, but it didn't take long for that thought to fly right out of his head.

The kiss pulled him right in.

Still, he couldn't deny that he wanted Rosalie more than his next breath. She clearly wanted him, too, and even though he should stop, he didn't.

Austin figured since he was about to jump right into a Texas-size mistake that he might as well make the most of it. Something that neither of them would ever forget. He slipped his hand around the back of her neck, dragged her closer and kissed her the way he'd been wanting to kiss her for days.

With nothing held back.

Her taste slid right through him like fire, and he brought her closer and closer until they weren't just plastered against each other, they were maneuvering to get themselves even closer.

That wasn't possible though with their clothes still on.

So Austin did something about that, too.

He slipped his hand beneath her top, unhooking the front clasp on her bra, and her right breast spilled into his hand. One touch, and he knew he had to have more. He shoved up her top and moved his kisses lower to her nipples.

Rosalie made a sound of pleasure, urging him closer all the while she fought with the buttons on his shirt. Soon she was touching his chest. Her hands on his bare skin. And coupled with the kisses, that only made him burn hotter.

Since her top kept slipping back down, Austin rid her of it, taking off her outer shirt and the tank top beneath it. Now he could kiss her without the barrier of her clothes, and it had exactly the effect he'd expected—it left both of them wanting a whole lot more, and he quickly figured out that this foreplay wasn't going to last nearly long enough.

"The bedroom," she managed to say.

Austin hadn't even thought to move this elsewhere, but it was a good idea in case Seth or someone else came into the cottage. So he scooped her up, and while the kisses raged on, he made his way to her bed. Talk about no finesse, but the moment her back touched the mattress, she pulled him down with her.

Everything sped up ever more. She tugged at his clothes. He tugged at hers. They sucked at it because they continued the maddening kisses, but he finally managed to strip off her jeans, dragging her panties off with them.

Oh, man.

The site of her naked robbed him of what little breath he had, and it drove home the realization that this wasn't going to last nearly as long as he wanted.

"Jeans," she said, her voice all silk and whispers. "Hurry."

Rosalie shoved down his zipper, touching him in the wrong place. Or rather the right one if he hadn't already been rock-hard and raring to go. He helped her with his jeans but mainly so he could get the condom from his wallet. Best not to make things worse by having unprotected sex.

Obviously, he wasn't moving fast enough for her because Rosalie tried to help with the condom.

Really not a good idea.

Especially since she kept repeating "hurry," and her touch was taking him many steps past the crazy stage. With that *hurry* repeating through his head, Austin eased into her.

And froze.

The sensations were too good. Too perfect. And even though his body was urging him on to hurry and finish this, to find the release for this need, he also paused just so he could savor the moment.

Rosalie looked up at him, her breath gusting. Her eyes wide. Her gaze focused solely on him. She opened her mouth, slowly, as if she might repeat that one word that'd driven them here to the bed.

But this time it wasn't *hurry* that she whispered.

It was his name.

Austin.

He held his breath, wondering if she had come to her senses and wanted to put an end to this. But, no. She pulled him back down, her mouth on his, for a kiss that fired his blood and his heart at the same time.

"Austin," she repeated in that same silky tone that she'd said *hurry.*

But hurrying wasn't necessary. That look, the sound of his name. The kiss. And being this close to her. All of that pinpointed until he had no choice but to move inside her.

Rosalie moved, too, going right into the rhythm of the strokes that would finally get them what they wanted.

Release.

Austin managed to snag her gaze at the moment that she climaxed. Her eyes were unfocused. Her breath wild. But he caught on to her chin and held the eye contact so he could watch her go over.

"Austin," she repeated.

No more hurry-up tone. Just Rosalie saying his name, just her urging him to join her as she fell.

So, that's what Austin did.

Chapter Fifteen

Rosalie braced herself for the slam of guilt that she was certain would come. Especially after that incredible climax with Austin.

But no guilt.

And, of course, that made her feel guilty.

Part of her—the logical, sane part—had known that this was coming. Austin and she had been skirting around this attraction for two days now, and with all the adrenaline and energy, it had to bubble over and send them straight to bed.

Which is exactly what it'd done.

They were both single. Both dealing with the same emotions from someone trying to kill them. The same search for the truth about her daughter and the baby farms. It was only natural that she would be lying beneath him and enjoying some nice little aftershocks of the climax. There was nothing wrong with it.

But the other part of her—the crazy, guilt-ridden part—also knew they'd landed in bed for all the wrong reasons.

Well, one wrong reason, anyway.

They shouldn't have carried things this far until they'd worked out their feelings for each other. She wasn't the sort who slept with a guy and then walked away, and she had to brace herself for a broken heart.

Because he might indeed do just that—walk away.

Austin, too, had to be dealing with the guilt of sleeping with his late partner's fiancée.

Or not, she amended, when he lifted his head, located her mouth and kissed her until Rosalie could have sworn she saw little gold stars. Of course, maybe that was just because the kiss went on for so long that she wasn't getting any oxygen to her brain.

Either way, it was an amazing kiss to top off what'd been an equally amazing experience.

"You said my name," Austin said, giving her that lazy smile that made her toes curl.

Yes, many times if she remembered correctly. "It seemed the right thing to say."

Rosalie smiled, too, hoping to keep the moment light. She wanted to hold on to this feeling just a little bit longer. Austin gave her another smile for a moment, too, but she could also see the worries in the shades of all that blue in his eyes.

"I don't want you to cry about this, about anything that has to do with us," Austin added as if choosing his words carefully. Which he probably was. He also likely figured that the ship had sailed on telling her not to feel guilty.

"No tears," she promised, but Rosalie wasn't sure it was a promise she could even keep.

Especially if Austin left.

That feeling came at her again. The one that made her feel as if someone had clamped on to her heart. She'd already lost so much, but the thought of losing Austin, too, just seemed, well, unbearable.

"I'll give you a minute." Austin dropped another of those mind-numbing kisses on her mouth and got off the bed to head to the bathroom.

Since she was suddenly aware that she was stark naked on the bed, Rosalie got up too and gathered her clothes that had been strewn over the room.

"No tears," Austin repeated, calling out to her from the bathroom.

Even if she had been on the verge of crying, it wouldn't have happened. Not after a butt-naked Austin stepped into the doorway.

Oh, mercy.

Why did just seeing him cause her to go all hot again? Maybe because he had a perfect body to go along with his other good attributes. Or maybe because she just couldn't seem to get enough of him.

"You're blushing," he pointed out.

"Because I'm gawking at you and wishing I could have you all over again."

Rosalie hadn't exactly intended to blurt that out, but she did like the way it caused the corner of Austin's mouth to lift into a sexy smile. He walked to her, that smile still on his face, and he reached for her. But reaching was as far as he got because his phone rang.

Just like that, Rosalie snapped out of her heated trance. The call could be about the investigation.

Or about Sadie.

Austin snatched his phone from his jeans pocket and started to dress while he took the call. What he didn't do was put it on speaker. Maybe because he was going to try to buffer any bad news they got.

But buffering wouldn't work.

"Who is this?" Austin asked the caller.

Rosalie hurried to him, as close as she could get so she could figure out what was going on.

The voice was mechanical, like one of those scramblers that kidnappers used.

Oh, God.

This had to be the person behind the baby farm. The person who might have Sadie.

Rosalie practically ripped the phone from Austin's hand and jabbed the speaker button.

"Are you two still listening?" the person asked.

"We're here," Austin answered. "Now, who are you and what the hell do you want?"

"I think I'll be the one to ask the questions," the person answered. The smugness came through even with the scrambler, and Rosalie wished she could reach through the phone lines and force this monster to give Sadie back to her.

"I need you to get the files and computers that were confiscated from Yancy's place," the caller continued. "Not just the flash drives, either, but the laptops in case anything is on the hard drives. Have someone bring them to you, then I'll tell you where I need you and Rosalie McKinnon to deliver them. Only the two of you. If you bring anyone else, the deal is off."

Austin and she exchanged glances. Yancy's things? Did that mean it was Yancy himself calling, or was this just another way to set him up? With everything that'd happened, neither option would surprise Rosalie.

"And why would I bring you Yancy's files and computers?" Austin demanded.

"Oh, didn't I mention that already? Must have slipped my mind." The smugness went up a notch. "We're working out a deal here, Agent Duran. You give me the items you took from Yancy's house—all of the items—and I'll give you something that you want real bad."

"What?" Austin snapped.

The silence crawled on until her stomach was clenched into a knot.

"I'll give you Rosalie's daughter, of course," the caller finally said. "She's here with me now."

And Rosalie heard something that sent her heart straight to her knees. It was a baby's voice, repeating a single word.

"Mama."

Chapter Sixteen

"I don't want you to do this," Austin said to Rosalie for the umpteenth time.

He figured he could say it a thousand times more and she still wouldn't listen.

The bad part about that?

Austin didn't blame her one bit. If that was his little girl out there, he wouldn't keep away, either. Still, he wanted Rosalie to stay safe, and delivering a "ransom" to a baby snatcher wasn't a good way to stay safe.

Especially since this particular ransom was fake.

The FBI hadn't gone along with the notion of removing what could be critical evidence in a multiple-felonies investigation, so Austin and Seth had come up with what they hoped would be enough to fool the kidnapper. They'd copied some of Yancy's business emails and such and made duplicates of some of the files.

Maybe it would be enough to get Sadie.

If this snake really had her, that is.

Austin wasn't even sure an eleven-month-old baby was capable of saying "Mama" or that it was proof that the baby was indeed Sadie. However, the simple repeated syllable had been more than enough to convince Rosalie that she was going through with this stupid plan.

At least now they had a drop point. The kidnapper had phoned again two hours after the first call and had demanded that Rosalie and Austin meet him at the site of the now-abandoned baby farm where Rosalie and he had worked undercover. It was remote, and there were plenty of places to hide.

Too many.

And that's why Rosalie's brothers Colt and Cooper had gone ahead of them to scope out the place from a distance. If the kidnapper had brought gunmen—and he or she almost certainly had—then Austin wanted to know what they were up against before they ever stepped foot on the place. Better yet, Austin wanted the hired guns eliminated so he could deal with this moron baby snatcher face-to-face.

Too bad the cops hadn't managed to locate Yancy or Vickie.

Austin would have liked to have tails on both of them. Or just have thrown them both in jail. However, they did have a tail on Sonny, and

Austin was getting text updates on the man. So far Sonny had gone into his room at the Sweetwater Springs hotel, and he hadn't come out. Maybe Sonny would stay there so they'd have one less suspect to worry about.

Of course, that didn't mean that Sonny hadn't hired gunmen to launch another attack. Or set up a ruse that could get Rosalie and him out into the open.

Like this one.

"No," Rosalie said when Seth tried to talk to her. "I'm going."

Seth was one of the most hardheaded people Austin had ever met, but he'd clearly met his match with Rosalie. Seth's jaw tightened, and his *do-something* gaze slashed to Austin.

Austin just gave a heavy sigh and shook his head. "She'll wait in the vehicle when we make the drop, and Colt, Cooper and you will stay out of sight so you can protect her."

That was the compromise Austin had finally made with Rosalie. After a heated *discussion*. She'd wait in a bullet-resistant car that the FBI used for dangerous undercover assignments. Seth would follow them to make sure they weren't attacked from behind. And Colt and Cooper would provide backup after they'd made the site as safe as possible.

Nothing about the plan was ideal, and it'd

take a miracle to pull it off. Still, it was the best possible plan under the worst possible circumstances.

Austin's phone buzzed, and he saw a text from Colt.

No one appears to be around. Will keep looking to make sure.

That was good. Except that Austin remembered those explosives and fires that'd been rigged at the second facility. It'd be hard for Colt and Cooper to check for that without putting themselves directly in harm's way, so that meant Austin had to keep watch for anything that could blow them all to smithereens.

Yeah, this was no piece-of-cake assignment.

Austin fired off a text to Colt. "Anything on infrared?"

Rosalie's brother had brought equipment that would detect the body heat of anyone nearby. It wouldn't give them the caller's identity, but it would be able to tell them how many hired guns they were up against.

"Nothing," Colt answered.

That was both good and bad. It meant gunmen weren't nearby. Well, unless they were using some kind of heat-shielding camouflage. Of course, there'd be no need for gunmen and camouflage if the plan was just to blow them up, and the infrared wouldn't detect any explosives.

"It's time," Rosalie said, glancing at the clock. Her hands were shaking.

Heck, she was shaking, and she couldn't seem to make herself stand still. She'd been pacing, fidgeting and trembling head to toe since the phone call from the kidnapper. Austin didn't expect any of those nerves to get better in the next hour or so.

"We need to leave," Rosalie added.

It's was only a twenty-minute drive to the site, and the drop-off time was forty-five minutes, but Austin understood her urgency to get out the door. Too bad that each moment outside put them in even greater danger. Of course, with their luck, the attacker could somehow launch explosives at the cottage if they stayed put.

"I'll drive slow," Austin said to Seth, knowing that Seth would do the same.

All of them were anxious to see if the kidnapper did indeed have Sadie, but it wasn't a good idea for them to stand around outside at the abandoned baby farm, waiting for this guy to show up. He or she could hurl explosives at them there, too, after getting the info from Rosalie and him.

Austin hurried her out to the car that he'd had Seth park directly outside the back door. Thanks to Seth, the fake files and computers were already on the backseat. They'd made a show of putting them there, too. Seth had brought in the fakes from the FBI office, so if anyone was watching the ranch, then maybe the stuff would appear to be the real deal.

It was nearly dark and bitterly cold. The wind was gusting, and Austin felt the flecks of sleet spit at him.

Great.

Now the weather was working against them. The roads would be slick, adding yet another level of danger to this already dangerous situation.

"I'm not stupid," Rosalie said when he pulled away from the ranch. "I know this is likely a trap, but I also know that in the past eleven months, this is the closest I've come to finding my baby."

Austin slid his hand over hers. It was about the only thing he could do to try to comfort her, and it wasn't much of a gesture. At least he didn't think it was much until her fingers closed around his for a quick squeeze.

It definitely gave him some comfort, anyway.

He glanced behind them to make sure Seth was following. He was, and he was keeping a safe distance so that it wouldn't readily appear that he was following them.

Of course, the kidnapper would be looking for something like that, and since the snake had been adamant about Rosalie and Austin coming alone, then he or she would be looking for any sign that they hadn't followed the rules and had brought backup.

Seth would have to drop way behind them when they approached the baby farm. And that was yet another part about this plan that Austin didn't like.

"Those photos are of Sadie," Rosalie continued several minutes later. "That means someone associated with this has her."

It did. But it didn't mean that person was going to hand Sadie over to them. Or that the person demanding the ransom was also the one who'd taken those photos.

Austin kept that to himself.

"If it isn't Yancy who's doing this," she went on, "then it's someone who wants to make him look guilty." Rosalie paused. "I'm hoping it's Yancy so we can put him behind bars for the rest of his life."

Yeah, Austin was hoping that, too, but maybe Vickie would be a less formidable foe. Except that Vickie could have hired just as much firepower as either Sonny or Yancy.

His phone buzzed. No text this time but an

incoming call, and the caller's name and number were blocked.

"The kidnapper." And Austin hit the answer button and put it on speaker.

"I see that you're on the way," the caller greeted them. "Lose Agent Calder though before you get here."

Austin mumbled some profanity. "You had the ranch under surveillance?"

"Of course. There's a lot at stake here."

There was. And that's why Rosalie's brothers had used binoculars to check if there was someone watching, but they hadn't spotted anyone. Still, that didn't mean the kidnapper hadn't managed to get a camera close enough to monitor their every move and could have been doing that for days. With all the ranch hands and workers on the sprawling McKinnon ranch, it wouldn't have been that hard to do.

"I'm guessing the sheriff and deputy are at the baby farm checking things out," the caller went on. He didn't wait for Austin to respond. "Good. They can stay there, and once you tell Agent Calder to take a hike, you can deliver those goods that the two of you put on the backseat of the car. How much trouble did the FBI give you about getting the stuff?"

"Plenty." And Austin hoped that meant that the kidnapper believed the evidence was real.

"You said the drop-off was the baby farm," he snapped.

And while the location sucked, Austin figured any alternative would suck even more.

"There's been a change of plans," the kidnapper said. It was that same smug tone that he'd used with his earlier calls. "Call Agent Calder now. Tell him to turn around and go back to the ranch."

"Why? So it'll be easier to kill us?" Austin came right out and asked.

"No. Because I don't want to make it easier for you to kill me. Especially since I'm holding the kid and all."

Rosalie sucked in a hard breath. "Don't you dare hurt my baby!"

"Wouldn't dream of it. She's my ticket to that evidence. Oh, and by the way, she's cute and sleeping like a baby for now. Keep it that way by following the rules. Ditch Calder and within five minutes, you'll have your kid."

Austin knew there was no way Rosalie could simply dismiss that as a lie. There was too much hope in her eyes to believe that she couldn't soon have her baby in her arms.

"Where are you?" Austin demanded of the kidnapper, but he was talking to himself because the caller had already hung up.

Cursing, Austin hit the end call button and

glanced in the rearview mirror at Seth's car. Then, he glanced at Rosalie.

"We have to do it," she insisted. "We have to tell Seth to stop."

Austin had a quick debate with himself, but he knew there was only one solution here.

And it was a bad one.

"Call Colt and Cooper first to give them our location. Then, call Seth," he finally said. "Tell him to pull off the side of the road until the kidnapper contacts us about the exchange."

Rosalie gave a shaky nod and made the calls in the order he'd told her. Cooper and Colt gave her a quick okay. Seth argued, of course, but he would do as they asked.

Austin hoped.

And while he was hoping, he added that maybe there was some way he'd be able to get Rosalie out of this alive while also rescuing Sadie.

Behind him, he saw Seth pulled to the side as they'd requested, but Rosalie's brother was also voicing his disapproval of the change in plans. However, Seth didn't get a chance to voice it for long because another call came in on Austin's phone.

"It's the kidnapper again," Rosalie said, quickly ending the conversation with her brother. As before, the screen showed that the caller ID had been blocked.

Austin automatically slid his hand over the gun in his shoulder holster. "What now?" Austin asked the moment Rosalie answered the call.

But the kidnapper didn't jump to answer. The moments crawled by, and if Austin hadn't heard the guy breathing, he would have thought no one was on the line.

"All right," the kidnapper finally said. He was still using the voice scrambler that made him sound like a cartoon character. "Agent Calder is far enough away so you can take the turn just ahead."

The windshield wipers were smearing the sleet on the windshield, so it took Austin a moment to see the road. Except it was more of a dirt-and-gravel path than an actual road. He eased on the brakes so he wouldn't go into a skid, and he made the turn.

Also slowly.

He turned on his high beams, hoping it would give him a better look of their surroundings. There were plenty of trees and shrubs. No houses. But just ahead he spotted a dark-colored SUV parked in the center of the path.

Rosalie took the gun from the glove compartment.

"Yeah, that's me," the kidnapper said. "Drive closer."

Austin didn't. He came to a full stop then and there.

"Rosalie stays in the car while you and I make the exchange," Austin insisted.

Again, the guy took his time answering. Maybe because he or she figured it would put them even more on edge. Austin wasn't sure it was possible to do that since every nerve and muscle in his body was on full alert.

"Suit yourself," the kidnapper finally said.

Austin hadn't thought it possible, but that indeed made him even more concerned. He'd expected an argument.

One that Austin was sure he would lose.

So, was this some kind of trap to get him out of the car so Rosalie could be kidnapped?

Or worse?

But if this bozo just planned to kill them, why hadn't he just started shooting? Maybe because the kidnapper suspected the car was bullet-resistant? Either way, there was nothing about this setup that Austin liked, and it just kept getting worse.

"I'll put the laptops and files on the side of the road where I'm parked," Austin said, trying a different angle. "Once that's done, you come and get it."

"Oh, I don't think that would be a good idea," the kidnapper answered. "It's the weather, you see. Wouldn't be good for the baby to be out for too long on a winter night like this. No. I'm thinking a better solution would be for you to drive closer. Less time outside for the kid."

But closer meant Rosalie and he would be easier targets.

"You haven't asked for proof that I've got the baby," the kidnapper added. "Well, here it is."

Austin didn't have to wait long this time. Only a few seconds. Before the interior light came on in the kidnapper's SUV. The light stabbed through the sleet and darkness, and even though Austin was parked a good thirty feet away, he had no trouble seeing the figures inside.

Two adults, both wearing dark clothes and ski masks.

And one of the masked adults was holding up a baby.

"Sadie," Rosalie said on a rise of breath, and she threw open the door.

Chapter Seventeen

Rosalie didn't even manage to get her foot out the door before Austin latched on to her shoulder and hauled her back into the car.

"I have to get to Sadie," she blurted out.

She heard the panic in her own voice. Felt it in every inch of her body, but she couldn't make herself stop. Everything inside her was screaming for her to get to her baby.

"You can't help Sadie if you're dead." Austin dragged her even closer to him and got right in her face. "Don't give them a reason to pull their triggers, not with the baby between them and you."

Sweet heaven.

She hadn't even considered that, but she did now. The threat of her own death didn't frighten her, but she couldn't bear the thought of doing anything to hurt Sadie. And if she stepped out there, those men might indeed try to shoot her because they thought she was some kind of loose end that needed to be tied up permanently.

Rosalie's gaze snapped back to the SUV ahead of them. The interior light went out, and she could no longer see the men or the baby. That didn't help with the panic and the nerves. At least if she could see Sadie, she would know that her little girl was all right.

Well, as all right as a baby could be while being held by kidnappers.

"Give her to me," Rosalie sobbed, knowing it wouldn't do any good. These monsters were using her precious baby as a bargaining chip. They didn't care that it was tearing her apart.

"Oh, you'll get her all right," one of the kidnappers said. "Just have Agent Duran drive closer and put the evidence in the covered plastic bin by our SUV. The sooner he does that, the sooner you'll get the kid."

And with that, he ended the call.

Rosalie couldn't think—her mind was a whirl of emotions and thoughts. She was about to ask Austin what they should do, but before she could say a word, he took the phone and texted Seth to give him their location and told her brother to approach on foot. Probably so the sound of his car engine wouldn't be detected. On foot though Seth might not get there soon enough to help them rescue Sadie, and he would be out in the open, possibly an easy target.

"We have to stall them," Austin said, easing the car close to the SUV. Not quickly. He inched along at a snail's pace. "We have to give Colt, Cooper and Seth time to get into place."

It made sense, but it also meant it would take even longer before she could get to her baby.

Austin kept driving, the car bobbing along on the uneven surface of the road, and he came to a stop a good ten yards from the SUV and a green plastic bin. He waited, glancing at the phone. Probably waiting to see if the kidnapper would order him to go even closer.

But no call came in.

"Stay put," Austin warned her, and he held eye contact with her again. Even in the dim light, she could see the warning he was giving her—*Don't go out there.*

Rosalie nodded.

"And keep watch all around us," Austin added. He put the car in Park, turned off the engine and the headlights. "I don't want anyone sneaking up on us."

She nodded again, and Rosalie lowered the window just a fraction so that she'd hopefully be able to hear anyone approaching their car.

Austin kept his gun in his right hand, and he stepped from the car, volleying his attention all around them, especially at the SUV where they were holding Sadie. He opened the back door and took out the first of the three laptops. Not quickly, either. He took his time getting a grip and moving it out of the vehicle and into the bin on the side of the gravel road.

His phone buzzed again. "It's the kidnapper," she relayed to Austin and hit the call button to put it on speaker.

"Hurry up for Pete's sake," the man snarled. "We don't have all night. You got two minutes to get that stuff out of the car, or we're driving off with the kid."

"No!" Rosalie practically shouted.

The kidnapper hung up but not before she saw something else in the interior of the SUV. The illumination from his phone was just enough that she could make out someone else in the backseat.

"There are three of them," she whispered to Austin.

Mercy, that didn't help with the panic. She was an okay shot, but the extra person meant that Austin and she were outgunned. Rosalie prayed that her brothers made it there soon. Maybe their sheer presence would be enough to get the kidnapper to surrender.

She could hope, anyway.

Austin picked up the pace of moving the

equipment while Rosalie kept her attention nailed to the kidnapper's SUV. Not that there was anything to see. But those seconds were ticking by. She wasn't sure if the man had been bluffing when he said they'd drive away, but it was a risk she couldn't take.

With the window down and the back door open, it didn't take long for the bitter cold to seep inside their own vehicle. The sleet was cutting like razors through the lights of the high beams, and the howling winter wind slapped at the tree branches, creating too much noise for her to hear much of anything.

The moment Austin finished moving the last of the laptops, his phone buzzed again, and when she answered it, Rosalie did hear the kidnapper's scrambled voice.

"It's too late," the voice said. That was it. The only warning she got before she heard the roar of the SUV's engine. The driver spun the car around, the tires digging into the soft ground on the side of the road.

What the heck was he doing?

But Rosalie soon got an answer to that when the driver hit the accelerator.

"No!" Rosalie shouted.

If the kidnappers even heard her, it didn't do any good.

Because the SUV sped away.

Austin's heart slammed against his chest. No. This couldn't be happening. Not when they were this close to getting Sadie from the kidnappers.

"Hurry!" Rosalie called out to him.

He did exactly that. Austin jumped back behind the wheel of the car and took off in pursuit.

Right now, every second was precious. He had no idea how long this particular ranch trail was, but he couldn't let the kidnappers make it out to a main road. If that happened, well, he couldn't go there.

"Why are they leaving?" Rosalie asked in between repeating for him to hurry.

"Maybe something spooked them." Like Seth, Cooper or Colt though Austin hadn't seen any signs of them. Austin pushed the accelerator hard. Going much faster than he should on the narrow, icy path. Still, it wasn't as if he had a lot of options here. He had to follow that SUV.

"Put on your seat belt," Austin warned Rosalie, "and stay down."

She did the first but not the second. Probably because she couldn't stop herself from watching the road ahead. She was also whispering a prayer.

They certainly needed a prayer or two.

Things were already bad, and there were plenty of things that could get even worse tonight. At least they were all alive. For now.

He had to maneuver the car through some tight curves on the uneven surface, and the trees and shrubs were so close to the path that they scraped like fingernails against the side of the car. The unnerving sound sure didn't help steady his breathing or heartbeat.

"If they're leaving the files and laptops behind," Rosalie said, "then maybe they didn't really want them in the first place."

Austin had already come to that conclusion. Not that he'd ever thought this was about the evidence. But he went back to his original idea. That maybe all of this had been staged to convince them that Yancy was behind this.

Or maybe Yancy believed by making himself look guilty that it would in turn make him appear innocent. A weird reverse psychology and exactly the sort of thing that Yancy would do to play with their heads.

Either way, this could have been a ruse to throw Rosalie and him off track. However, that didn't answer the question about the baby.

"You're sure it was Sadie in the SUV?" he asked while he fought the steering wheel to stay on the road.

"I'm sure." She didn't hesitate, either.

That was enough verification for Austin. He never discounted gut feelings, even when a gut feeling could be leading them right smack dab into the middle of danger.

He took another sharp curve and immediately had to hit the brakes. The SUV was there, parked, not on the road this time but about twenty yards away in the center of a small clearing. The headlights were off, ditto for the interior light, and it was hard to tell if anyone was inside.

Austin hoped like the devil that they hadn't ditched the vehicle and used another trail to get out. If so, it'd be darn hard to find them since he wouldn't even have a description of a secondary vehicle.

"Don't get out," Austin reminded Rosalie, and this time she stayed put. Both of them stared at the SUV, waiting, while keeping watch around them. "Maybe the kidnapper will call soon."

But soon didn't happen.

The seconds dragged on, giving Rosalie and him plenty of time to think of all the bad things that could happen in the next couple of minutes.

"If they've already left, we need to know," Rosalie finally said.

Yeah. And the longer they waited, the farther away the kidnappers could get. If they were indeed fleeing, that is. If not, well, that was a chance Austin was about to have to take.

"Wait here, and I mean it," he repeated, taking his phone from her and shoving it into his pocket. Then he gave her a quick kiss. "There's a burner cell in the glove compartment. Use it to call Seth if anything goes wrong."

She took hold of his arm when he reached for the door. "Was that a goodbye kiss?"

"I hope not."

"Well, it felt like one." Her breath broke, and Rosalie leaned toward him and returned the kiss. "Swear to me that it won't be a goodbye."

Even though time definitely wasn't on their side right now, he took a moment to make eye contact with her. "I promise," Austin said.

At best, it was wishful thinking.

At worse, an out-and-out lie because it was a promise he had no control over keeping. Once he stepped out there, he was essentially a sitting duck with at least three hired guns in the area.

Still, he stepped out. And Austin kept his gun ready. It was impossible to stay behind cover, but he used the trees, skirting around them to make his way to the SUV. Eventually, though, he would have to step out into that clearing and hope that Seth and the others would soon arrive for backup.

"Are you there?" Austin called out to whoever might be in that SUV.

No answer.

He glanced back at the car to make sure Rosalie was staying put. She was, thank God. And he hurried even closer to the SUV and ducked behind a scraggly mesquite. Not much cover, but if the kidnappers had wanted to shoot him, they'd already had ample opportunity.

"I left the files and laptops on the road," Austin went on while he inched closer.

The windows on the SUV were heavily tinted, and there wasn't even a moon for him to see shadows inside. However, if Rosalie was right, there were three of them. Plus, the baby. And the baby meant despite his having his gun ready, that the last thing he'd be doing was firing shots.

Maybe the kidnappers were on the same page.

Austin pulled in a long breath and stepped out from the tree. He didn't charge forward. Best not to look as if he were on the attack. However, he was still a good five yards from the SUV when he heard something he didn't want to hear.

Movement near the car.

He shifted in that direction, hoping that he didn't see Rosalie hurrying toward him.

But he saw something much worse.

She was out of the car all right, and someone was behind her.

That someone had a gun pointed at Rosalie's head.

Chapter Eighteen

Rosalie heard the sound behind her a split second too late. She felt someone hook an arm around her neck. Before she could even react or shout out a warning to Austin, the person snapped her back and pressed a gun to her temple.

"Move and you die," he growled in a whisper right against her ear.

And there was no mistaking that it was a *he*. The person wasn't using a voice scrambler, and the hard muscles of his chest pressed against her back.

"Rosalie!" Austin called out, and while using the trees for cover again, he started to race toward her.

"Wouldn't do that if I were you," the man said, taking aim at Austin and then cursing him when he apparently didn't have a clean shot. "Could be bad for her health."

Without the scrambler, Rosalie had no trouble recognizing the voice.

It was Sonny.

All of the events of the past eleven months started to whirl through Rosalie's head. Was this the monster responsible for taking her daughter, or was Sonny just a hired thug? She desperately wanted to know the answers, but more than that, she wanted Austin and her baby safe.

"The cops were watching you," she said to Sonny. "You were in your hotel room."

"Was," he corrected. "I slipped out the back."

Not good. The other cops in Sweetwater Springs didn't know he was here.

With his gun aimed, Austin ducked behind a tree about ten yards away. "Let her go," he ordered.

"Can't do that. She's coming with me for now." Even though she couldn't see Sonny, she felt him move slightly, maybe glancing around. "I might let her go as soon as I have the situation with her brother contained."

Oh, God. Seth. They weren't going after him, too. She prayed Seth would be able to stay safe.

"What does her brother have to do with this?" Austin asked.

"I figure he's nearby. Or he soon will be. Too soon for me to get out of here with both him and you on my tail. Rosalie can help with that."

Sonny was taking her hostage. To use her as

a human shield so he could try to stop or even kill Seth and Austin.

It was well below freezing, and her teeth started to chatter. She was shaking, her breath seemingly frozen in her lungs. Still, she had to focus on what had to be done here. And what had to be done was getting her hands on Sadie.

"Where's my baby?" Rosalie asked.

"She's nearby, too. You'll get to see her soon enough. All you have to do is cooperate and come with me. I'll take you both somewhere so you can live out a long, happy life."

She desperately wanted to believe him, but it was hard to believe a man with a gun at her head.

Austin leaned out, shook his head. "You have no intentions of letting either Rosalie or me walk away from this."

Sonny lifted his shoulder. Definitely not a denial. But then, Sonny probably figured that Austin and she knew way too much to let them go. They didn't. Well, other than knowing that Sonny was almost certainly part of the baby farms.

"Did you shoot yourself so you'd look innocent?" Austin asked. Rosalie realized he'd moved closer.

"No, one of my employees accidentally did that when we were trying to clear out of the second baby farm. But I thought it was a nice touch. It got me in the back of your truck that night, didn't it?"

Yes, it had, and on that entire drive to the hospital they'd been riding with a coldhearted monster.

"Why did you take my baby?" she asked, not in a whisper, either. She was hoping for the sound of her voice to cover any sounds that Austin might make. Also, it might give her brother a warning that something was wrong.

Again, Sonny looked around. "When I was working for Yancy, his wife asked me to help with an adoption. She wanted a kid, and I'd heard about an operation that dealt in black market babies. I decided to start one of my own. Two of them, in fact. But thanks to you two, I had to blow up one of the places."

So, Sonny was the one who'd set up the baby farms. Or at least the two near Silver Creek.

"Yancy wanted Rosalie's baby?" Austin asked. Again, he'd moved.

"No, that idiot had no idea what was going on. I targeted Rosalie's baby so if things went wrong, then Yancy would be the patsy, and the proof of it would be that he was the one who had the kid."

Rosalie had to clamp her teeth over her bottom lip to stop herself from screaming. "But you tried to kill Yancy at the hospital."

"Another nice touch, huh? Wasn't really trying to kill him, but after that, it put Yancy at the top of your list of suspects, didn't it?"

It had, and Austin's and her distrust and hatred for Yancy had made it even easier to suspect him. Of course, Sonny had been a suspect, too. For all the good it'd done them. Here they were with Sonny calling the shots.

For now.

Maybe Austin or even Seth could soon do something about that. Maybe she could, as well. If she managed to drop down, then perhaps that would give Austin a clean shot. Of course, if she failed, both of them could die.

"And you continued the ruse of setting up Yancy by having us bring his files and computers," Rosalie concluded. She wanted to learn all she could in case they needed it to put this monster behind bars. Of course, for that to happen, they needed to get that gun out of his hands.

"Yep," Sonny readily admitted. "I used Yancy's computer to set up the baby farms. There are hidden files on them. Nothing that Yancy would have found, but I figured the FBI wouldn't have any trouble. Also figured you'd bring me fake computers. No way would the FBI let something like that out of their hands."

Sonny was right about that, too. So, that meant this was all designed to lure Austin and her out so they could be killed. And now, she might get Seth killed, too, unless Austin could get close enough and at the right angle to stop Sonny.

"Who has my baby?" she asked Sonny.

"She's safe and with one of my employees. Don't worry. She's been well taken care of all these months."

Rosalie felt Sonny's muscles go stiff.

"Agent Duran, you need to stay put," he growled, "or Rosalie dies before seeing her kid. You wouldn't want that, would you?"

The thought of seeing her baby even for a few moments caused her heart to soar. But the feeling didn't last long. Rosalie didn't want Sonny to kill her in front of Sadie. Her baby was too young to know what was going on, but still the nightmare might stay with her for the rest of her life.

"Did someone adopt Sadie?" she asked, and Rosalie prayed that she could live with the answer. "Did Yancy's ex-wife get her?"

"No." Sonny looked around again. "After Yancy's marriage went south, I decided to sell the kid to another buyer, but that deal fell through. Then, things heated up with the baby farm investigation, and I figured it best if I kept the kid in case something went wrong. And it did."

"There's no reason to hold on to her now," Rosalie insisted, though she knew nothing that she said to him would do any good. He'd committed so many criminal acts that she figured his heart was untouchable.

"Yeah, there is. As long as I have her, your badge-carrying family will back off."

Sweet heaven. He planned to keep using Sadie. Not that she'd expected anything less, but it turned her blood to ice to hear it spelled out.

"Where's Yancy?" Austin called out. He seemed close. Maybe close enough to do something.

"In hiding." Sonny chuckled, clearly amused about that. "All the evidence will point to him looking very guilty, and he's trying to cover his butt. He'll surface soon enough, I'm sure, and the FBI can arrest him."

Yes, with evidence that Sonny had faked. She wanted Yancy behind bars, but not like this.

"What about Vickie?" Rosalie asked. "Was it really her in the photo, and does she have my baby?"

"Nope to both. I was telling the truth when I said she was innocent in all of this. The photo was just to get you looking in her direction and to muddy the waters. She's great in the sack but not very bright. I wouldn't have trusted her to be a real part of this. Look how she ran when just a little thing went wrong."

That little thing involved Austin's nephew.

That created a new surge of rage inside her. Sonny was playing a dangerous game with innocent lives. Without thinking, she drew back her elbow and rammed it into Sonny's stomach. In the same motion, she dropped to the ground, hoping that Austin had a shot.

Cursing, Austin leaned out and fired.

But so did Sonny.

The shots blasted through the air.

AUSTIN DUCKED BEHIND the tree, barely dodging Sonny's shot, but Austin's own shot missed, too.

He cursed.

This was exactly what Austin had been trying to prevent. Rosalie being caught in the middle of gunfire. Worse, Sonny dropped down, too, trying to grab hold of Rosalie again, and in doing so it took out any chance that Austin had of a second shot.

Austin raced toward them, trying to position himself between Rosalie and Sonny, but it was already too late for that. Sonny managed to keep hold of her, and he slung her between them.

Using her as a human shield.

Since Sonny didn't have complete control of

his gun, Austin went after the man's hand so that he couldn't aim it at Rosalie. That cost him big-time because Sonny punched him, hard. So hard that Austin could have sworn something in his head exploded, and for a few crucial seconds, it robbed him of his breath.

That didn't stop Austin.

He went after Sonny again, and this time managed to land a punch of his own.

Rosalie twisted and squirmed, trying to get out of the fray, but Austin couldn't help her because he had his hands full with Sonny.

"Back away from him!" someone shouted.

Austin got just a glimpse of a muscle-bound man hurrying from the SUV. Great. One of Sonny's hired guns, no doubt. He didn't need this, and Austin slammed his gun against Sonny's head so he could put an end to this before the goon made it to them.

The bash to the head caused Sonny to fall back. But the man didn't stay down. He reached out, latched on to Rosalie's hair and pulled her back in front of him. He put his gun to her head again.

Hell. That wasn't the way Austin had wanted this to play out.

Austin scrambled behind one of the trees so that Sonny wouldn't gun him down. He couldn't save Rosalie if Sonny killed him.

"Let's try this one more time," Sonny snarled. "Move and she dies real fast."

Sonny's breath was ragged, and his face was bleeding. Austin figured he looked about the same. Thankfully, the only bright spot in all of this was that Rosalie didn't seem to be hurt.

Austin needed to do something fast to keep it that way.

"I was trying to do her a favor by letting her see the kid," Sonny added, glancing around him again.

"I doubt that," Austin argued. "You're not the do-a-favor type. I'm guessing you want Rosalie alive so you can draw Seth out. I'm also guessing that you're afraid Seth won't let this go once Rosalie disappears."

Sonny smiled. "Can't leave a bulldog like Calder out there. While I'm at it, those other three brothers of hers will have to go, as well. Yancy'll get the death penalty for all of their deaths. Yours, too."

Rosalie made a sound, anger mixed with fear, and Austin shook his head, a warning for her not to throw another elbow. This time, Sonny might just pull the trigger.

"You had a chance to kill us the night we picked you up in my truck," Austin reminded him.

"That would've been too soon. Had to figure

out first what you two knew and if you'd told anyone anything that could lead back to me. Had to keep you close. And now that I've figured it out, you both know way too much to keep drawing breath."

"We didn't have a confirmation of who owned the baby farms," Austin insisted. "Not until tonight."

"Yeah, but you would have figured it out soon enough. Agent Calder's not the only bulldog in these woods. You would have kept coming until you got to the truth, and that truth would have put me behind bars."

If Austin had his way, it would do more than that. Sonny would get the death penalty because Austin knew for a fact that some of the birth mothers had been murdered at the baby farm.

"You okay, boss?" the thug asked, coming even closer.

"Yeah." Sonny spit out a mouthful of blood. "Stay close but check on Hutchins. He should have been here by now."

Austin didn't know the man. The name hadn't come up in the investigation, but he guessed this was another hired gun.

One who'd been sent to find Seth.

Maybe Seth, Cooper and Colt would be able to evade this Hutchins and the second goon. Austin needed that to happen because he intended to do whatever it took to get Rosalie out of this.

And he saw his chance when the hired gun walked away to go after Seth.

"Don't do anything stupid," Sonny said, probably because he knew that Austin was about to do something. "I have another *helper* in the SUV. This one has some long-range shooting skills, and since I'm not too concerned now about keeping Rosalie alive much longer, my man will pull the trigger."

Austin made a split-second glance behind him, but as before he couldn't see inside the SUV. With all the scheming that Sonny had done, though, it wouldn't surprise him if several hired guns were in there.

There was a sound to his left, maybe footsteps. Maybe Seth. However, before Austin could even look in that direction, he heard another sound.

The SUV door opening.

Hell. He didn't need another guy with a gun getting in on this. But it wasn't a man. It was a gray-haired woman, and she was clutching what appeared to be a baby in a blanket.

"You said the baby wouldn't be in danger!" the woman shouted. With that, she turned and ran straight for the woods.

A man jumped out from the SUV. The rifleman, no doubt, and he volleyed glances between his boss and the woman.

"Go after her!" Sonny shouted. "And when you find her, kill her and bring me the kid."

Chapter Nineteen

"No!" Rosalie shouted, and she would have tried to go after the woman if Sonny hadn't yanked her back by her hair.

Pain shot through her, but it was nothing compared with the pain stabbing through her heart. The woman had Sadie, Rosalie was sure of it, and if the hired gun found her as Sonny had ordered, Sadie might be hurt, too.

And even if the woman managed to get away, it was possible that Rosalie would never see her baby again.

That couldn't happen.

This had to end tonight so she could be reunited with Sadie.

"I have to see her," Rosalie tried again, and she fought, squirmed and did whatever she could to try to break loose of Sonny's grip.

"Let her go," Austin ordered, stepping out from cover and putting him in the direct line of fire.

Sonny immediately turned his gun on Austin. And fired. Thank God Austin got out of the way in time.

"Sonny!" someone shouted before he could take aim at Austin again. Whoever it was, the person sounded as if he was running straight toward them.

"Hutchins," Sonny mumbled.

One of his hired guns. The one who was supposed to be out there hunting down Seth. She'd hoped her brother had managed to take care of him, but apparently not.

Did that mean Hutchins had managed to kill Seth?

Rosalie choked back a gasp and the tears. None of that would help her now. Only escaping would do that, and then she could get the baby and find Seth.

Her gaze connected with Austin when he looked out from the tree. Too bad they weren't mind readers because if they could work together, they might be able to come up with a plan that wouldn't get them both killed.

Austin had been right about one thing. If Rosalie died, it could have devastating consequences for Sadie. Either Austin or she had to stay alive to make sure Sadie lived.

Mercy, though, it hurt to think of losing Austin. He didn't deserve this. He'd made her fight his own, and he was out here because of her. Because he cared for her.

Rosalie's feelings went a lot deeper than that.

She was in love with him.

And it was the worst time possible for her to realize that. Maybe she would get a chance to tell him.

"It's me. Don't shoot," Hutchins warned Sonny, and several moments later, the man reached them. He had a bulky build and was wearing a black ski mask that he'd partially lifted up on his face.

"We got a big problem, boss," Hutchins said. "Leon's dead. I found him just up the road. Somebody had snapped his neck."

"Hell." And Sonny repeated it. "I sent him to check on you. Where the devil is Calder?"

Hutchins shook his head. "I don't know. Don't know about the other two lawmen, either. If they're out there, they're keeping quiet."

That caused Sonny to spew another round of raw profanity. "Find them. Kill them."

The death order had barely left Sonny's mouth when there was a sound that Rosalie didn't want to hear.

A gunshot.

Even if it was one of her brothers doing the shooting, she didn't want the bullets fired around the baby. She also didn't want Seth, Cooper or

Colt hurt, but she knew it was possible that the shot had been aimed at any one of them.

While he kept a firm grip on her hair, Sonny pulled her behind a tree and moved a small communicator on his coat collar so that it was closer to his mouth. "Hendricks?" he said into the piece.

Nothing.

Rosalie wasn't sure, but she was guessing this was the goon who'd gone after the nanny.

"Hendricks?" Sonny repeated not just into the communicator, but he shouted out the man's name.

"Won't do any good to yell for him," someone yelled. "I just put a bullet in him."

Yancy.

What the heck was he doing here? Rosalie couldn't see him, but judging from the sound of his voice, he was in the woods where she'd last seen the nanny and baby.

Oh, God. Had Yancy done something to them?

"What the hell do you want, Yancy?" Sonny snarled.

"Figured that'd be kinda obvious. I'm here because you're trying to set me up. Not gonna happen. I didn't have anything to do with those kidnapped brats."

Rosalie didn't know where to aim her anger,

but she was actually glad that Yancy had eliminated the man going after the nanny. One hired gun down, but she had no idea how many others there were.

Plus, now they had to contend with Yancy. Even though he appeared to be there to stop Sonny, she didn't trust him. He could try a reversal of Sonny's plan and kill them all, setting it up so that Sonny looked guilty.

"This isn't your fight," Sonny yelled back to Yancy. "Leave now, and you won't get hurt."

"Well, you see, I'm thinking this is my fight." Yancy sounded like his usual cocky self. "Now, I don't care a rat's butt if Rosalie and Austin get killed in the process, but, Sonny-boy, you're about to meet your unholy maker."

That was the only warning they got before Yancy started shooting.

AUSTIN LAUNCHED HIMSELF at Rosalie to pull her to the ground so he could get her out of the path of Yancy's shots.

But Sonny beat him to her.

Sonny scrambled behind one of the trees and dragged Rosalie with him. Why, Austin didn't know. Sonny had plans to kill Rosalie and him, anyway, but maybe he didn't want his enemy to get that *privilege*.

Yancy's shots slammed into the tree that

Sonny and Hutchins were using for cover with Rosalie. However, Yancy also sent a few Austin's way. Since Yancy had already killed the hired gun who'd gone after the nanny, or so he'd claimed, then it was clear he didn't intend to leave any witnesses behind.

Austin stayed low and looked around, hoping to catch a glimpse of Seth, Cooper or Colt. If they were out there—and he was pretty sure they were since someone had broken the other thug's neck—then they were keeping well hidden. Austin hoped they were close enough in case he needed backup for what he was about to do.

And what he was about to do was get Rosalie the heck out of there.

That was the first step, and then they had to go after the nanny. Unless there was another vehicle nearby, then it meant the woman was out in the freezing-cold woods with a baby. Plus, there was the likelihood that Sonny had other hired guns out there. Ones who'd worked the baby farm for him.

In other words, goons who would do anything, including murder.

Another of Yancy's bullets slammed into the tree just above Austin's head. Since the man wasn't taking time to reload, he'd obviously come with multiple weapons. Still, he'd eventually run out of ammo unless he, too, had brought significant backup with him.

A strong possibility.

Sonny and his man were doing their own share of returning fire, and while they were occupied with Yancy's attack, Austin inched his way toward Rosalie. She had her head down, thank God, but she was also looking in his direction. Obviously waiting for him to put his plan of escape into motion.

Except the plan was a thin one.

Basically, Austin intended to grab Rosalie, head to the bullet-resistant car and, once he had backup in place, the search for the nanny and the baby could begin.

"Move back," Austin mouthed to her, hoping that Rosalie could understand what he was saying.

Hutchins understood it all right. The hired gun pivoted, turning his weapon on Austin.

The shots came fast.

So fast that it took Austin a moment to realize that Hutchins hadn't been the one to pull the trigger.

The shot had come from Yancy.

And the bullet hit Hutchins squarely in the chest. Obviously a kill shot because Hutchins crumpled to the ground without making a sound.

"You're gonna pay for that!" Sonny shouted.

He came out from the tree, his gun already aimed at Yancy, and started firing.

Nonstop.

Austin took advantage of the moment and hurried to Rosalie. He hooked his arm around her waist to get her moving just as he heard a too-familiar sound. One of the bullets slamming into someone. He made a quick glance over his shoulder.

That someone was Yancy.

The man made a guttural sound of raw pain, falling. His gun dropped right along with him.

Sonny didn't waste a moment savoring his victory of killing an old foe. He whirled around, turning his gun on Austin and Rosalie. They scrambled behind a boulder in the nick of time.

Another shot came their way. Then another. Sonny took cover behind the tree again, protecting himself and keeping them pinned down at the same time.

Since his heartbeat was already crashing in his ears, it took Austin a moment to hear something else. And this time it was a welcome sound.

Sirens.

Lots of them.

Rosalie's brothers had come through with

plenty of backup. But would the cops arrive in time? Sonny's shots were coming way too close.

Since Austin was covering Rosalie's body with his, he could feel her knotted muscles. Could hear her ragged breathing. She'd come way too close to dying—again—and there was still time for Sonny to try to get off one more deadly shot.

That's what Austin had to prevent.

"I love you," she said.

At least that's what Austin thought she said. But he had to be wrong about that.

Didn't he?

Like the earlier kiss, maybe this was her way of saying goodbye, but he sure as hell wasn't ready to say goodbye to her.

"Rosalie? Austin?" someone called out.

Seth.

He sounded close enough to help Austin put an end to this.

"Over here," Austin shouted back just as he levered himself up a little and fired a shot at Sonny.

Sonny jumped back behind cover and sent another shot Austin's way. Austin braced himself for another hail of bullets. Sonny's last-ditch attempt to take them out before he turned his killing efforts on Seth.

But that didn't happen.

"This isn't over," Sonny said, adding some vicious profanity.

And he took off running.

SINCE ROSALIE WAS flat on the ground, at first she didn't understand why Austin practically jumped off her. And then she lifted her head and saw what was happening.

No!

Sonny was getting away, and worse, he was running in the same direction as the woman with the baby. If Sonny caught up with them, he might carry through on his death order, and the baby could be hurt in the process.

"We have to stop him," Rosalie insisted.

Even though Austin tried to take her by the arm and stop her, she threw off his grip and instead got him moving after Sonny.

"There might be other gunmen out there," Austin reminded her.

The thought of it spiked her heart even more, but she couldn't let Sonny take this fight to Sadie. Thankfully, Austin must have understood that because he finally gave up struggling with her and moved ahead of her so he could quicken the pace.

"We're here!" Austin shouted over his shoulder.

Rosalie glanced back and saw Seth running after them.

Good.

They might need an extra gun or two before this was over. Also the sirens were close now, probably right on the road where Austin had left the car. If there were any of Sonny's goons on that side of the clearing, Cooper and Colt could take care of them.

Austin didn't wait for Seth to catch up. He kept her moving until they reached a thick clump of trees, and he pulled her behind them with him.

"Sonny could be waiting somewhere to ambush us," Austin whispered.

That put her heart right back in her throat. It was exactly the sort of thing that scum like Sonny would do. Still, they couldn't just stand there and wait because if his plans weren't to ambush them, then he was escaping.

That couldn't happen.

If he got away, the danger would just continue, and worse, she might never get Sadie back. If Sonny managed to get his hands on Sadie again, he would no doubt make sure Rosalie never found her.

Austin and she waited, the wind and the sleet swiping at them. Mercy, it was so cold, and her baby was out there in this with a killer on her trail.

"Any sign of Sonny?" Seth asked when he hurried into the trees with them.

Austin had to shake his head. All of them were breathing through their mouths now. All of them on edge and primed for a fight.

"We can't wait any longer," she insisted, figuring she would get an argument from at least one of them.

She didn't.

Austin motioned for Seth to go to the left, and he motioned for her to follow him to the right. They fanned out, looking and listening for any sign of Sonny or another of his hired guns.

Both Austin and Seth turned on their phones and used the light to have a look at the ground. Rosalie didn't see anything, but Austin must have because he gestured at Seth again, and they took off, heading deeper into the woods.

Rosalie tried to pick through all the sounds. The bitter wind, their footsteps crunching onto the icy ground and her own heartbeat. She hoped to hear something that would help them find Sadie.

But there was nothing.

They just continued to work their way through the clutter of trees and shrubs while Austin followed some kind of tracks that she couldn't even see.

"It'll be okay," Austin whispered to her.

It took her a moment to realize the reason he said that was because she had a death grip on his shoulder. Rosalie eased back her fingers a little, but there was nothing she could do to ease the tension in her body.

Or forget what she'd said to Austin earlier.

I love you.

Judging from the look he'd given her, he'd been just as surprised by it as she had been.

But it was true.

It had taken their near deaths for her to come to that realization, and the timing couldn't have been worse. When this was over and Sadie and everyone else was safe, Rosalie needed to make sure that her saying "I love you" didn't mean anything.

Well, nothing except that she meant it and would probably get her heart broken.

Austin hadn't given her even a hint that he was ready for a relationship. Yes, they'd had sex, but again, that'd happened after yet another nightmare attack. She didn't want that to have been the reason he'd landed in bed with her, but she had to accept that it had played a big part in it.

And that his feelings weren't the same as hers.

Soon, after she had her baby in her arms, she could work that all out. If Austin wanted to work it out, that is. It was entirely possible that once

Sadie was safe and Sonny was behind bars, that Austin would leave and go back to his own life.

That didn't help soothe her thoughts any.

Of course, there was nothing about this situation that was *soothing*. They were literally on a life-and-death run to save her baby, and if they didn't get lucky, it was a race they might lose.

They kept moving, the air so cold that she thought maybe her breath had frozen. Austin finally stopped, lifted his hand and pointed toward a pair of oaks just ahead.

Seth nodded.

Rosalie didn't immediately see what had captured their attention. Not until she caught a glimpse of the movement. It looked to be the sleeve of a man's coat.

Maybe Sonny's.

She expected Seth and Austin to move closer to try to capture him. But they didn't. They stayed put, their gazes firing all around them.

And she soon figured out why.

The rush of movement came from their right. A blur of motion.

Sonny.

He ducked behind some shrubs but not before Rosalie saw that he wasn't wearing a coat. That meant he'd likely planted his coat as some kind of trap to lure them out. Thank God Austin and

Seth hadn't fallen for it because her instincts had been to go after it and find Sonny.

"Get all the way down on the ground," Austin whispered to her.

It was an effort with her tight, frozen muscles. The moment Rosalie managed to do as he'd said, Austin took off.

Sweet heaven.

She hadn't expected that and didn't want him running right into the path of Sonny's gun.

There were footsteps to her left, and while her brother stayed low, Seth made his way to her. He hovered over her, waiting. Rosalie waited, too, and each second seemed to take an eternity. It sickened her to think of Austin out there, trying to finish this fight, but there was no other choice. She wondered if he knew just how thankful—and terrified—she was that he was willing to risk everything.

"What the hell?" Sonny snarled.

She lifted her head just enough to see Austin launch himself at the man. He'd obviously circled around Sonny and sneaked up on him. Now they were in the middle of another fight.

"Stay here," Seth told her, and he raced toward Austin and Sonny.

There was no way she could stay put, but Rosalie did keep cover behind the trees as she made her way toward Seth and Austin. She certainly didn't want to get close enough to Sonny to let him grab her and use her as a human shield again.

However, she saw something that caused the skin to crawl on the back of her neck.

Sonny had his gun aimed right at Austin.

"No!" she screamed, and she bolted toward them.

Maybe Sonny hadn't expected her to be so close. Or for her scream to be so loud. Either way, he glanced over at her.

It was just a split second.

But it was enough of a distraction for Austin to knock the gun from Sonny's hand. He didn't stop there. Austin shoved him onto the ground and put his own gun right against Sonny's throat.

"Give me a reason to pull this trigger," Austin said, his voice dripping with the emotion of the nightmare that this monster had put them through.

Rosalie walked even closer despite Seth's attempts to stay between her and Sonny. But she wanted to get a look at Sonny's face.

And she did.

He was smiling.

If Seth hadn't caught on to her, Rosalie would have gone after Sonny to punch him. Or at least she would have tried to do that. How dare this

SOB smile after what he'd done to them and so many other families.

"You didn't win," Sonny said, staring at her.

That sent an even icier chill through her. "What do you mean?" she asked at the same time that Austin said, "Ignore him. He'll say anything to get to you because he knows he'll be spending the rest of his life behind bars."

"Yeah," Sonny readily agreed. Still smiling. "But even behind bars, I still win."

Austin hauled Sonny to his feet and used the plastic cuffs that Seth handed him to restrain the man. "How do you figure that?" Austin asked.

"Easy. The woman who had the baby? The nanny," Sonny clarified. "She has orders, and I know for a fact she'll carry them out, especially after what she saw tonight. She'll be afraid for the baby, and she would have headed to the other car that we left just up the trail."

Rosalie put her hand on her chest because it felt as if her heart might beat out of her chest. "What do you mean?" she repeated. "Where is she?"

Sonny's smile stretched across his face. "The nanny is leaving the country as we speak, and she's been given the money and the resources to disappear for good." His smile turned to a taunting laugh. "You'll never see your daughter again."

Chapter Twenty

Austin wanted to believe Sonny was lying about the nanny disappearing with Rosalie's baby. After all, Sonny hadn't told the truth about much else. But this was exactly the kind of stunt a man like him would pull.

The nanny wouldn't be around to testify against him.

And there'd be no absolute proof that he'd ever had Sadie kidnapped. Unless there was some kind of DNA evidence in the car, that is, but Austin was betting Sonny had made sure there wasn't.

"Where's the nanny?" Austin demanded.

Sonny just kept on smiling. A bad mistake. Because Austin didn't even try to hang on to his temper. He punched Sonny in the face. Sonny's head flopped back, and even with the blood spreading across his mouth and teeth, he managed to keep that damn smile.

"Please," Rosalie begged, and Austin could hear every bit of the agony in her voice.

Agony that was clearly giving Sonny pleasure. Since he'd been captured and was about to spend the rest of his life in jail, he wanted Rosalie to have that same life sentence.

"Give me some time alone with him," Seth said. Unlike his sister, there was only one emotion in his voice.

Rage.

Seth would likely beat Sonny within an inch of his life. Austin wanted to do that himself, but time was precious right now, and he didn't want to spend that time trying to get answers from this piece of slime.

"The airport," Austin said. "If she's leaving the country, that's where she'll go. And Sweetwater Springs has a small airport that's only about ten miles away."

That finally got the smile off Sonny's face. Austin hoped that meant he'd hit pay dirt. Of course, he could be doing that to taunt them, to get their hopes up.

Seth took out his phone. "I'll call the airport and see if there are any flights about to leave. If so, I'll have them stop the plane from taking off."

Rosalie shook her head. "But what if she goes somewhere other than Sweetwater Springs?"

"I'll call Colt and have him help," Seth explained. "Cooper and he are out here in the woods looking for the nanny and any other thugs this idiot might have brought with him. If they both start making calls, then we should be able to stop her from getting away."

Good. Austin wanted all the help they could get.

"Go to the local airport," Seth insisted. "If the nanny's not there, if she's headed to San Antonio instead, we'll stop her."

Austin didn't hesitate to take Seth up on his offer. Neither did Rosalie. They started running back toward the car. It seemed to take an eternity to get there, but the second they were inside, Austin started the engine and got them moving.

He hadn't thought it possible, but the roads seemed even slicker than before. Maybe that would work for them.

"The nanny cared about the baby," Austin reminded Rosalie. "She wouldn't have run if she hadn't. And that means she'll take care driving on these roads."

It could slow the woman down just enough for Austin to catch up with her. Of course, there was another obstacle once they had the nanny and the baby.

What if the little girl wasn't Sadie?

Austin wasn't sure Rosalie would be able to

handle that. Wasn't sure he could, either. He didn't know Sadie. Had never held her in his arms the way Rosalie had, but it would crush him to have her disappear.

He didn't want to think about what it would do to Rosalie.

"Seth should have called by now," she mumbled.

She sounded on the verge of panicking, and he couldn't blame her. The stakes were sky-high right now, and with the road conditions, they were still about eight minutes out from the airport.

"Back in the woods, you told me that you loved me," he said.

Yeah, the timing sucked for this particular conversation, but it might stop them both from losing their minds. Or maybe it would just add to it, he amended when he saw the flash of surprise in Rosalie's eyes.

"You didn't mean it," he concluded. "I get it. Adrenaline. Heat-of-the-moment kind of thing—"

"I meant it."

Oh.

That gave him a jolt of emotions. All good ones. Despite the hell they'd just been through, he found himself smiling. Judging from Rosalie's expression, that didn't help settle her nerves.

"It doesn't make things better," Rosalie continued before he could gather his thoughts and answer her. "Nor easier. Just the opposite—it complicates things. And for the record, I don't expect you to return the feelings. In fact, I'm not sure I want you to."

Well, that caused his smile to go south. Austin shook his head, sure he was missing something that should be obvious.

"You don't want me to love you?" he came right out and asked.

She huffed.

Yep, this clearly fell into the obvious category, and he was too thickheaded to figure it out. He was about to ask her to spell things out for him, but his phone rang, and he saw Seth's name on the screen when he took it from his pocket. So that he could keep both hands on the steering wheel, Austin put the call on speaker and gave the phone to Rosalie.

"Please tell me you're close to the airport," Seth snapped.

"About three or four minutes out. Why?" And judging from the sense of urgency in Seth's voice, Austin was afraid he wasn't going to like the answer.

"Because there's a small plane about to take off, and I believe the nanny and baby are on it."

"Oh, God," Rosalie mumbled. "Were you able to stop it?"

"Yeah, but there might be another problem. There's a lone air traffic controller running the place this time of night, and he just radioed for the pilot to abort takeoff. That doesn't mean the nanny won't just get off the plane, get back in the car and head elsewhere."

Rosalie repeated that *Oh, God.*

"I'm hurrying," Austin assured Seth. He ended the call so he could focus on getting them to the airport in one piece.

The sleet kept coming at them, pelting the windshield and making it hard to see. It didn't help that Rosalie's breath was gusting now, much as it'd been when she was facing down a killer like Sonny.

Of course, these stakes were even higher now.

She could lose her baby forever.

Austin took the turn to the airport. Too fast. But thankfully, he didn't go into a skid. He managed to keep the car on the road, heading straight toward the small metal hangar that sat just off the runway. The moment he pulled in front of it, he saw the plane.

Thank heaven.

It hadn't taken off, but the engine was still running. If necessary, he'd drive the car in front of the plane to stop it from taking off.

"There," Rosalie said, pointing to the side of the hangar.

Austin looked in that direction and spotted an SUV, similar to the one that Sonny had used to get to the woods. There was white steam coming from the exhaust pipe, which meant that engine, too, was on.

Before Austin could bring his car to a full stop, Rosalie bolted out, making a beeline toward the SUV.

"Wait!" Austin called out to her, but just as he'd expected, she didn't listen. Too bad because Sonny could have a hired gun waiting in there.

Or worse.

Maybe the nanny wasn't even here at the airport with the baby. Maybe this was another of Sonny's tricks to lure them to a spot where they could be gunned down. It wouldn't get him off the hook with the felony charges, but Sonny might take pleasure in their suffering.

Austin threw the car into Park, drew his gun and got out so he could hurry after Rosalie. However, before he could get to her, she yanked open the SUV door on the driver's side.

And she froze.

Austin could have sworn his heart froze, too, because he was terrified that she was looking down the barrel of a killer's gun. He got his own gun ready and took aim the moment that he came to a stop.

But it was no killer staring back at them.

It was the woman they'd seen in the woods. Midfifties with gray hair and a thin build. She was alone. Well, maybe. She certainly wasn't holding the baby, and there was no thug in the seat next to her.

That put a knot in Austin's gut.

Until he glanced in the back and saw the infant seat. It was facing the rear of the SUV, and he couldn't tell if it was empty or not, but he'd soon remedy that. Austin threw open the rear door.

And there she was.

A beautiful sleeping baby.

She was snuggled into thick blankets, and because the car's heater was on high, she didn't appear to be cold.

"Don't hurt her," the woman insisted, and she jumped from the car to try to push Austin away. He held his ground, but she just kept on pushing despite the fact he outsized her and was armed.

"He won't hurt her," Rosalie said. "We're here to save her."

She eased onto the backseat next to the baby. With her fingers trembling, she reached out and touched the baby's hand. Rosalie's breath hitched in her throat, and the tears came. Austin wanted to go to her, to hold her, to share what he hoped was about to be a happy reunion, but he had some business to settle first.

"Who are you?" the woman demanded.

"Austin Duran, and this is Rosalie McKinnon. Now, who the heck are you?" He used his FBI tone even though he wasn't sure it was necessary. The woman seemed to be trying to protect the baby, and her size didn't make her much of a threat.

"Laura Keels," she said, and her wary gaze went from him to Rosalie. Austin expected her to try to stop Rosalie from touching the baby, but she didn't. "Did you say your name was McKinnon?" she asked.

Rosalie nodded, but she didn't take her attention off the baby. She eased the baby from the seat and took her into her arms.

"McKinnon," the nanny said once more, and she turned to grab something from the car.

Austin didn't let that happen. He caught on to her and put her against the door the way he would any criminal suspect.

"I don't have a gun," she insisted. "But I do need to show you something. It's in my wallet in the diaper bag on the passenger's seat."

There was indeed a diaper bag on the seat, and while he didn't see a weapon, he had no intentions of letting her get to her wallet to show them anything. Not yet, anyway.

"I need answers. Why were you working for a man like Sonny?" Austin asked.

She frantically shook her head. "I didn't know he was violent. I didn't know he'd done anything wrong. Please tell me he's under arrest."

"He is."

It was hard to tell if Laura was telling the truth, so he motioned for her to continue.

"I'm a nanny. I've been one for over thirty years, and when Sonny contacted a former employer and offered me a job, I took it. He brought me the baby eleven months ago, and I've had her ever since. I've cared for her just as I would all the babies I've loved and raised over the years."

"And you didn't wonder if the baby had been kidnapped or stolen?" Austin snapped.

Rosalie kept the baby cuddled in her arms, but she looked up at Laura, obviously waiting for the answer to that.

"Of course not," Laura insisted. "Sonny said the baby's father was a drug lord. A very dangerous man. And that the baby's mother had gone into hiding and that she'd be back to claim the child when it was safe."

Austin huffed. "You believed that?"

"I didn't have any reason not to." Laura paused, her own tears now streaming down her cheeks. "Not until tonight. Not until I saw what a violent man Sonny really was. He said we were only going to see the baby's mother. I didn't know there'd be guns and shooting."

"Did Sonny hurt the baby?" Rosalie asked. "Did he touch her?"

Laura's eyes widened. "No. God, no. I would have never let that happen. I cared for her, kept her safe until she could be reunited with her mother."

Rosalie swallowed hard. "I believe I am her mother."

He braced himself for Laura to deny that. But she didn't. She looked at him again. "I need to get something out of my wallet. It's something you need to see."

Austin kept his gun on her and finally nodded. Laura didn't make any fast moves, probably because he didn't seem too friendly, and once she'd taken the wallet from the diaper bag, Laura pulled out what appeared to be a small strip of plastic.

Thanks to the interior lights of the car, he saw that it was the kind of bracelet that hospitals put on newborns. It was pink and there was something written on it.

McKinnon Baby Girl.

"Room 112," he read from the bracelet along with the date.

Sadie's birthday.

Rosalie's breath shattered, and the sound she made—relief mixed with joy—caused the baby to stir.

"It's Sadie," Rosalie managed to say. She pressed a flurry of kisses on the baby's face. "That's the date she was born, and that's the room I was in at the hospital. She's mine. She's really mine."

Yeah. They would need to do a DNA test, of course, but it would only verify what they already knew. That this was Rosalie's daughter.

Just as a mom would do with a newborn, Rosalie eased back the blanket, checking for fingers and toes. They were all there, and Sadie looked like a perfectly healthy child.

"I took care of her," Laura repeated. "She's a good baby, but I always knew that she needed her mom and dad. You'll take good care of her, too."

It wasn't a question, but Austin nodded. No doubt about it. He would take care of her and Rosalie.

If Rosalie let him, that is.

He clearly had some things to work out with her, especially that part about her not wanting him to love her. Austin still wasn't sure how to get around that.

His phone rang. It was Seth, again. And

Austin realized he should have already called him with an update since Seth would be worried about his sister. The reunion had obviously distracted him.

"Rosalie's fine," Austin said the moment he answered. "We found the nanny in time." And he had to clear away the lump in his throat when he saw the way that Rosalie was looking at her daughter. "The baby is Sadie."

Seth made a sharp sound of relief. "You're sure?"

"Yeah, we have proof."

Another sound of relief. "How's Rosalie handling that?"

"About the way you'd think." Her face was practically glowing from the love that was there. "The nanny's still here, and I'm hoping once you're finished booking Sonny that you can take her statement."

"Colt and Cooper can deal with this sack of slime," Seth insisted. "Oh, and I just got off the phone with headquarters. You'll get the collar for Sonny so you'll be getting your badge back. My advice is to take a day or two, though."

That wasn't even on Austin's radar right now, but he was sure later he'd appreciate that. Especially since working out of the San Antonio office would keep him close to Rosalie.

And he'd definitely take that time off, maybe more than a day or two.

"I'm on the way to have that chat with the nanny," Seth said, and with that, he hung up.

Good. Austin was glad that Seth would help tying up the loose ends because he had something of his own that he had to finish. He started with Laura.

"I need to check you for weapons," he said, figuring he wouldn't find any. And he didn't. Nor did the woman object to the search. When he was done, he tipped his head to the hangar.

"Wait in there. Agent Calder from the FBI will be here soon to ask you some questions."

She shook her head again, and new tears sprang up. "I swear I didn't know I was doing anything wrong."

"That's what you need to tell Agent Calder. He'll take your statement, and if you know anything that can add to our case against Sonny, then tell him that, too."

Though more wouldn't be necessary. Sonny had confessed to so many felonies that he'd be locked away for life. As a minimum. But if they could also pin Janice's murder on him, then he might get the death penalty.

Laura gave a shaky nod, started toward the hangar but then looked into the car at Rosalie. "Can I kiss her goodbye?" Laura asked.

He could see Rosalie think about it, probably because she wasn't ready to give up another moment with her baby, but she finally motioned for Laura to come closer. The nanny leaned down and kissed the top of Sadie's head.

"She doesn't like peas but loves country music," Laura added to Rosalie. "If she gets fussy at night, just put on George Strait. That'll soothe her right down. Oh, she can crawl anywhere, fast, and I think she might be walking by the new year."

Rosalie hung on to each word. Precious little bits of information for things that'd she wanted to know about her baby.

"I think that's everything, but if you got any questions, I'll give Agent Calder my number so you know how to get in touch with me."

Rosalie nodded.

"Be a good girl for your mama," Laura said softly to the baby.

Sadie smiled. "Mama."

That put some fresh tears in Rosalie's eyes, too.

"I taught her to say that," Laura explained, "because I figured one day you'd finally get to see her, and you'd want to hear her say it to you."

Rosalie's breath fluttered. "I do. Thank you for taking such good care of her."

The women's gazes met, and Laura brushed

a kiss on Rosalie's cheek, as well, before she started toward the hangar. The moment she was away from them, Austin got into the car with Rosalie and Sadie and closed the door. Not because he thought Laura was a threat but because he wanted to keep Sadie warm.

Sadie turned and looked at him. Studying him, actually, as if trying to figure out who he was. At least she didn't seem frightened of him.

"I'm Austin," he said, though it seemed silly to introduce himself to a baby.

Still, Sadie must have liked it because she smiled at him, and he could have sworn that his heart doubled in size. Man, how was it possible to love someone this much after just one look at her?

Rosalie looked at him, smiled, too, and kissed Sadie's fingers when the baby touched Rosalie's mouth. "Thank you for helping me find her."

You're welcome was the standard response, but Rosalie and he were well past that.

He hoped.

"You said you didn't want me to love you," Austin reminded her.

Surprise flashed through Rosalie's eyes, and she fumbled with whatever she was trying to say to him.

Austin decided to help her along with that fumbling. "I think you meant you didn't want me to feel obligated. And I don't. It wasn't obligation, the danger or the spent adrenaline that had me taking you to bed."

Everything stilled, as if the earth itself was holding its breath and waiting for him to finish. Rosalie was certainly waiting, and her mouth had dropped open a little. Sadie was touching his chin. All in all, it was a perfect moment to say what he wanted to say.

"Rosalie, I took you to bed because I'm in love with you."

There it was, all out in the open.

Well, almost.

"And I want you to marry me so that you, Sadie and I can be a family," Austin added.

Rosalie kept staring at him, her mouth still open.

Sadie playfully pinched his nose.

Then, Rosalie's breath swooshed out, and she moved so fast to kiss him that Austin didn't even see it coming. But he sure as heck felt it. That kiss did a lot more than just warm him from head to toe. It gave him the answer he wanted. Still, Austin needed to hear the words.

"Will you marry me?" he repeated with his mouth still against Rosalie's.

She kissed him, but he could feel her smiling while she did it. "I love you with all my heart, so my answer is yes. Yes. Yes. I'll marry you."

He would have been happy with just one yes, but he did like her enthusiasm.

Apparently, so did Sadie, because she clapped her hands.

It was yet another perfect moment. Austin was betting there'd be plenty more times just like this one.

A lifetime of them, in fact.

He gathered Rosalie and Sadie into his arms and was ready to start that new life with both of them.

* * * * *

Look for more books in USA TODAY
bestselling author Delores Fossen's
Sweetwater Ranch *miniseries in 2015.*
You'll find them wherever
Harlequin Intrigue books are sold.

LARGER-PRINT BOOKS!

HARLEQUIN *Presents*

PASSION
GUARANTEED
SEDUCTION

GET 2 FREE LARGER-PRINT NOVELS PLUS 2 FREE GIFTS!

YES! Please send me 2 FREE LARGER-PRINT Harlequin Presents® novels and my 2 FREE gifts (gifts are worth about $10). After receiving them, if I don't wish to receive any more books, I can return the shipping statement marked "cancel." If I don't cancel, I will receive 6 brand-new novels every month and be billed just $5.05 per book in the U.S. or $5.49 per book in Canada. That's a saving of at least 16% off the cover price! It's quite a bargain! Shipping and handling is just 50¢ per book in the U.S. and 75¢ per book in Canada.* I understand that accepting the 2 free books and gifts places me under no obligation to buy anything. I can always return a shipment and cancel at any time. Even if I never buy another book, the two free books and gifts are mine to keep forever.

176/376 HDN F43N

Name _____ (PLEASE PRINT) _____

Address _____ Apt. # _____

City _____ State/Prov. _____ Zip/Postal Code _____

Signature (if under 18, a parent or guardian must sign)

Mail to the Harlequin® Reader Service:
IN U.S.A.: P.O. Box 1867, Buffalo, NY 14240-1867
IN CANADA: P.O. Box 609, Fort Erie, Ontario L2A 5X3

Are you a subscriber to Harlequin Presents books and want to receive the larger-print edition? Call 1-800-873-8635 today or visit us at www.ReaderService.com.

* Terms and prices subject to change without notice. Prices do not include applicable taxes. Sales tax applicable in N.Y. Canadian residents will be charged applicable taxes. Offer not valid in Quebec. This offer is limited to one order per household. Not valid for current subscribers to Harlequin Presents Larger-Print books. All orders subject to credit approval. Credit or debit balances in a customer's account(s) may be offset by any other outstanding balance owed by or to the customer. Please allow 4 to 6 weeks for delivery. Offer available while quantities last.

Your Privacy—The Harlequin® Reader Service is committed to protecting your privacy. Our Privacy Policy is available online at www.ReaderService.com or upon request from the Harlequin Reader Service.

We make a portion of our mailing list available to reputable third parties that offer products we believe may interest you. If you prefer that we not exchange your name with third parties, or if you wish to clarify or modify your communication preferences, please visit us at www.ReaderService.com/consumerchoice or write to us at Harlequin Reader Service Preference Service, P.O. Box 9062, Buffalo, NY 14269. Include your complete name and address.

HPLP13R

LARGER-PRINT BOOKS!
GET 2 FREE LARGER-PRINT NOVELS PLUS
2 FREE GIFTS!

HARLEQUIN®

Romance

From the Heart, For the Heart

YES! Please send me 2 FREE LARGER-PRINT Harlequin® Romance novels and my 2 FREE gifts (gifts are worth about $10). After receiving them, if I don't wish to receive any more books, I can return the shipping statement marked "cancel." If I don't cancel, I will receive 4 brand-new novels every month and be billed just $4.84 per book in the U.S. or $5.24 per book in Canada. That's a savings of at least 19% off the cover price! It's quite a bargain! Shipping and handling is just 50¢ per book in the U.S. and 75¢ per book in Canada.* I understand that accepting the 2 free books and gifts places me under no obligation to buy anything. I can always return a shipment and cancel at any time. Even if I never buy another book, the two free books and gifts are mine to keep forever.

119/319 HDN F43Y

Name _____ (PLEASE PRINT)

Address _____ Apt. #

City _____ State/Prov. _____ Zip/Postal Code

Signature (if under 18, a parent or guardian must sign)

Mail to the **Harlequin® Reader Service:**
IN U.S.A.: P.O. Box 1867, Buffalo, NY 14240-1867
IN CANADA: P.O. Box 609, Fort Erie, Ontario L2A 5X3
Want to try two free books from another line?
Call 1-800-873-8635 or visit www.ReaderService.com.

* Terms and prices subject to change without notice. Prices do not include applicable taxes. Sales tax applicable in N.Y. Canadian residents will be charged applicable taxes. Offer not valid in Quebec. This offer is limited to one order per household. Not valid for current subscribers to Harlequin Romance Larger-Print books. All orders subject to credit approval. Credit or debit balances in a customer's account(s) may be offset by any other outstanding balance owed by or to the customer. Please allow 4 to 6 weeks for delivery. Offer available while quantities last.

Your Privacy—The Harlequin® Reader Service is committed to protecting your privacy. Our Privacy Policy is available online at www.ReaderService.com or upon request from the Harlequin Reader Service.

We make a portion of our mailing list available to reputable third parties that offer products we believe may interest you. If you prefer that we not exchange your name with third parties, or if you wish to clarify or modify your communication preferences, please visit us at www.ReaderService.com/consumerschoice or write to us at Harlequin Reader Service Preference Service, P.O. Box 9062, Buffalo, NY 14269. Include your complete name and address.

LARGER-PRINT BOOKS!
GET 2 FREE LARGER-PRINT NOVELS PLUS
2 FREE GIFTS!

HARLEQUIN®

super romance®

More Story...More Romance

YES! Please send me 2 FREE LARGER-PRINT Harlequin® Superromance® novels and my 2 FREE gifts (gifts are worth about $10). After receiving them, if I don't wish to receive any more books, I can return the shipping statement marked "cancel." If I don't cancel, I will receive 6 brand-new novels every month and be billed just $5.69 per book in the U.S. or $5.99 per book in Canada. That's a savings of at least 16% off the cover price! It's quite a bargain! Shipping and handling is just 50¢ per book in the U.S. or 75¢ per book in Canada.* I understand that accepting the 2 free books and gifts places me under no obligation to buy anything. I can always return a shipment and cancel at any time. Even if I never buy another book, the two free books and gifts are mine to keep forever.

139/339 HDN F46Y

Name _____ (PLEASE PRINT) _____

Address _____ Apt. # _____

City _____ State/Prov. _____ Zip/Postal Code _____

Signature (if under 18, a parent or guardian must sign) _____

Mail to the **Harlequin® Reader Service:**
IN U.S.A.: P.O. Box 1867, Buffalo, NY 14240-1867
IN CANADA: P.O. Box 609, Fort Erie, Ontario L2A 5X3

Are you a current subscriber to Harlequin Superromance books and want to receive the larger-print edition?
Call 1-800-873-8635 today or visit www.ReaderService.com.

* Terms and prices subject to change without notice. Prices do not include applicable taxes. Sales tax applicable in N.Y. Canadian residents will be charged applicable taxes. Offer not valid in Quebec. This offer is limited to one order per household. Not valid for current subscribers to Harlequin Superromance Larger-Print books. All orders subject to credit approval. Credit or debit balances in a customer's account(s) may be offset by any other outstanding balance owed by or to the customer. Please allow 4 to 6 weeks for delivery. Offer available while quantities last.

Your Privacy—The Harlequin® Reader Service is committed to protecting your privacy. Our Privacy Policy is available online at www.ReaderService.com or upon request from the Harlequin Reader Service.

We make a portion of our mailing list available to reputable third parties that offer products we believe may interest you. If you prefer that we not exchange your name with third parties, or if you wish to clarify or modify your communication preferences, please visit us at www.ReaderService.com/consumerschoice or write to us at Harlequin Reader Service Preference Service, P.O. Box 9062, Buffalo, NY 14269. Include your complete name and address.

HSRLP13R

ReaderService.com

Manage your account online!

- Review your order history
- Manage your payments
- Update your address

> *We've designed*
> *the Harlequin® Reader Service*
> *website just for you.*

Enjoy all the features!

- Reader excerpts from any series
- Respond to mailings and special monthly offers
- Discover new series available to you
- Browse the Bonus Bucks catalog
- Share your feedback

Visit us at:

ReaderService.com